The River Girl's Song

Angela Castillo

ISBN: 1511705310
ISBN-13: 978-1511705318

To all the women of the world,
who have cried quiet tears,
and whispered silent prayers,
and fought private battles.
You are the warriors
that make this world go 'round.

Acknowledgments

Many thanks to the mayor of Bastrop, Texas, Ken Kesselus, for his passionate study of our town and his effort to make those studies available to anyone who is interested. Thank you to Pioneer Farm in Round Rock, Texas, for allowing me to come and experience pioneer life for myself. And thanks to my mom, Charisse Haines, and my Grandma, Donna Eckwall, for being examples of enduring and amazing women of spirit and strength.

JULY 1886

1

Scarlet Sunset

"We need to sharpen these knives again." Zillia examined her potato in the light from the window. Peeling took so long with a dull blade, and Mama had been extra fond of mash this month.

Mama poured cream up to the churn's fill line and slid the top over the dasher. "Yes, so many things to do! And we'll be even busier in a few weeks." She began to churn the butter, her arms stretched out to avoid her swollen belly. "Don't fret. Everything will settle into place."

"Tell that to Jeb when he comes in, hollering for his dinner," muttered Zillia. The potato turned into tiny bits beneath her knife.

"Don't be disrespectful." Though Mama spoke sharply, her mouth quirked up into a smile. She leaned over to examine Zillia's work. "Watch your fingers."

"Sorry. I wasn't paying attention." Zillia scooped the potato bits into the kettle and pulled another one out of the bag. Her long, slender fingers already bore several scars reaped by impatience.

"Ooh, someone's kicking pretty hard today." Mama rubbed her stomach.

Zillia looked away. When Papa was alive, she would have given anything for a little brother or sister. In the good times, the farm had prospered, and she chose new shoes from a catalogue every year. Ice was delivered in the summer and firewood came in two loads at the beginning of winter. Back then, Mama could have hired a maid to help when the little one came.

She and Mama spent most of their time working together, and they discussed everything. But she didn't dare talk about those days. Mama always cried.

"I might need you to finish this." Mama stopped for a moment and wiped her face with her muslin apron. "I'm feeling a little dizzy."

"Why don't you sit, and I'll make you some tea?" Zillia put down her knife and went to wash her hands in the basin.

Water, streaked with red, gushed from beneath Mama's petticoats. She gasped, stepped back and stared at the growing puddle on the floor. "Oh dear. I'm guessing it's time."

"Are you sure?" Dr. Madison said you had weeks to go." Zillia shook the water off her hands and went to her mother's side. She'd helped with plenty of births on the farm, but only for animals. From what she'd gathered, human babies brought far more fuss and trouble.

Mama sagged against Zillia's shoulder, almost throwing her off balance. She moaned and trembled. The wide eyes staring into Zillia's did not seem like they could belong to the prim, calm woman who wore a lace collar at all times, even while milking the goats.

Zillia steadied herself with one hand on the kitchen table. "We need to get you to a comfortable place. Does it hurt terribly?"

Mama's face relaxed and she stood a little straighter. "Sixteen years have passed since I went through this with you, but I remember." She wiped her eyes. "We have a while to go, don't be frightened. Go tell your stepfather to fetch the doctor."

Zillia frowned, the way she always did when anyone referred to the man her mother married as her stepfather. Jeb had not been her choice. He was no kin to her. "Let me help you into bed first."

They moved in slow, shaky steps through the kitchen and into Mama's bedroom. Zillia hoped Mama couldn't feel her frenzied heartbeat. *I have no right to be afraid; it's not me who has to bring an entire baby into this world.*

Red stains crept up the calico hem of Mama's skirts as they dragged on the floor.

A sourness rose in the back of Zillia's throat. *This can't be right.* "Is it supposed to be such a mess?"

"Oh yes." Mama gave a weak chuckle. "And much more to come. Wait until you meet the new little one. It's always worth the trouble."

Mama grasped her arm when they reached the large bed, covered in a cheery blue and white quilt. "Before you go, help me get this dress off. Please?"

Zillia's hands shook so much she could hardly unfasten the buttons. It seemed like hours before she was able to get all forty undone, from Mama's lower back to the nape of her neck. She peeled the dress off the quivering shoulders, undoing the stays and laces until only the thin lace slip was left.

Another spasm ran through Mama's body. She hunched over and took several deep breaths. After a moment, she collected herself and stumbled out of the pile of clothing.

When Zillia gathered the dress to the side, she found a larger pool of blood under the cloth. Thin streams ran across the wood to meet the sunlight waning through the windowpanes. "There's so much blood, Mama, how can we make it stop?"

"Nothing can stop a baby coming. We just have to do the best we can and pray God will see us through."

"I know, Mama, but can't you see... I don't know what to do." Zillia rubbed her temples and stepped back.

Mama's mouth was drawn, and she stared past Zillia, like she wasn't there.

Mama won't want the bed ruined. Zillia pulled the quilt off the feather tick and set it aside. A stack of cloths had been stored beneath the wash basin in preparation for this day. She spread them out over the mattress and helped her mother roll onto the bed.

Thin blue veins stood out on Mama's forehead. She squeezed her eyes shut. "Go out and find Jeb, like I told you. Then get some water boiling and come back in here as fast as you can."

Zillia grabbed her sunbonnet and headed out the door. "God, please, please let him be close. And please make him listen to me," she said aloud, like she usually prayed.

Parts of her doubted the Almighty God cared to read her thoughts, so she'd speak prayers when no one else could hear. At times she worried some busybody would find out and be scandalized by her lack of faith, but unless they could read thoughts, how would they know?

None of the urgency and fear enclosed in the house had seeped into the outside world. Serene pine trees, like teeth on a broken comb, lined the bluff leading to the Colorado River. Before her, stalks littered the freshly harvested cornfield, stretching into the distance. Chickens scattered as she rushed across the sunbaked earth, and goats bounded to the fence, sharp eyes watching for treats.

"Let Jeb be close!" she prayed again, clutching her sunbonnet strings in both fists. She hurried to the barn. Her mother's husband had spent the last few days repairing the goat fence, since the little rascals always found ways to escape. But he'd wanted to check over the back field today.

Sounds of iron striking wood came from inside. She released the breath she'd been holding and stepped into the gloomy barn.

Jeb's back was towards her, his shirt soaked through. Late summer afternoon. A terrible time for chores in Texas, and the worst time to be swollen with child, Mama said.

"Jeb, Mama says it's time. Please go get the doctor."

"Wha-at?" Jeb snarled. He always snarled when her mother wasn't around. He swung the axe hard into a log, so it bit deep and stuck. The man turned and wiped the sweat from his thin, red face. Brown snakes of hair hung down to his shoulders in unkempt strands. "I got a whole day of work left and here it is, almost sunset. I don't have time to ride into town for that woman's fits and vapors. She ain't due yet."

Zillia fought for a reply. She couldn't go for the doctor herself; she'd never leave Mama alone.

Jeb reached for the axe.

"There's blood all over the floor. She says it's time, so it's time." Zillia tried to speak with authority, like Mama when she wanted to get a point across. "You need to go Jeb. Get going now."

When it came to farm work, Jeb moved like molasses. But the slap came so fast Zillia had no time to duck or defend herself. She fell to the ground and held her face. Skin burned under her fingers.

"Please, Jeb, please go for help!" she pleaded. Though he'd threatened her before, he'd never struck her.

"Shut up!" Jeb growled. "I'll go where and when I wish. No girl's gonna tell me what to do." He moved away, and she heard the horse nicker as he entered the stable.

Wooden walls swirled around Zillia's head. The anger and fear that coursed through her system overcame the pain and she pushed herself up and stood just in time to see Jeb riding down the road in the direction of the farm belonging to their closest neighbors, the Eckhart family.

They can get here faster than the doctor. First commonsense thing the man's done all day. "Please God," she prayed again. "Please let Grandma Louise and Soonie be home."

Blood, scarlet like the garnets on Mama's first wedding ring, seemed to cover everything. The wooden floor slats. Linen sheets, brought in a trunk when their family came from Virginia. Zillia's fingers, all white and stained with the same sticky blood, holding Mama's as though they belonged to one hand.

The stench filled the room, sending invisible alarms to her brain. Throughout the birth, they had played in her head. *This can't be right. This can't be right.*\

The little mite had given them quite a tug of war, every bit as difficult as the goats when they twinned. At last he'd come, covered in slippery blood that also gushed around him.

Over in a cradle given to them by a woman from church, the baby waved tiny fists in the air. His lips opened and his entire face became his mouth, in a mighty scream for one so small. Zillia had cleared his mouth and nose to make sure he could breath, wrapped him in a blanket, and gone back to her mother's side.

Mama's breaths came in ragged gasps. Her eyelids where closed but her eyes moved under the lids, as though she had the fever. Zillia pressed her mother's hand up to her own forehead, mindless of the smear of red it would leave behind.

The burned sun shrank behind the line of trees. No fire or lantern had been lit to stave off the darkness, but Zillia was too weary to care. Her spirits sank as her grasp on Mama's hand tightened.

At some point Mama's screams had turned into little moans and sobs, and mutterings Zillia couldn't understand. How long had it been since they'd spoken? The only clock in the house was on the kitchen mantle, but by the light Zillia figured an hour or more had passed since Jeb left. When the bloody tide had ebbed at last, Zillia wasn't sure if the danger was over, or if her mother simply didn't have more to bleed.

A knock came at the door. The sound she had waited and prayed for, what seemed like all her life. "Please come in." The words came in hoarse sections, as though she had to remind herself how to speak.

The door squeaked open and cool evening air blew through the room, a blessed tinge of relief from the stifling heat.

"Zillia, are you in here?" A tall, tan girl stepped into the room, carrying a lantern. Her golden-brown eyes darted from the mess, to the bed, to the baby in the cradle. "Oh, Zillia, Jeb met Grandma and me in town and told us to come. I thought Mrs. Bowen had weeks to go, yet." She set the light on the bedside table and rushed over to check the baby, her moccasins padding on the wooden floor.

"No doctor, Soonie?" Zillia croaked.

"Doctor Madison was delivering a baby across the river, and something's holding up the ferry. We passed Jeb at the dock, that's when he told us what was going on. The horses couldn't move any faster. I thought Grandma was going to unhitch the mare and ride bareback to get here."

Despite the situation, Zillia's face cracked into a smile at the thought of tiny, stout Grandma Louise galloping in from town.

An old woman stepped in behind Soonie. Though Grandma Louise wasn't related to Zillia by blood, close friends called her 'grandma' anyway. She set down a bundle of blankets. A wrinkled hand went to her mouth while she surveyed the room, but when she caught Zillia's eye she gave a capable smile. "I gathered everything I could find from around the house and pulled the pot from the fire so we could get this little one cleaned up." She bustled over to the bedside. "Zillia, why don't you go in the kitchen and fill a washtub with warm water?"

Though Zillia heard the words, she didn't move. She might never stir again. For eternity she would stay in this place, willing her mother to keep breathing.

"Come on, girl." Grandma Louise tugged her arm, then stopped when she saw the pile of stained sheets. Her faded blue eyes watered.

Zillia blinked. "Mama, we have help." *Maybe everything will be all right.*

Grandma Louise had attended births for years before a doctor had come to Bastrop. She tried to pull Zillia's hand away from her mother's, but her fingers stuck.

Mama's eyes fluttered. "Zillia, my sweet girl. Where is my baby? Is he all right?"

Soonie gathered the tiny bundle in her arms and brought him over. "He's a pretty one, Mrs. Bowen. Ten fingers and toes, and looks healthy."

A smile tugged at one corner of Mama's pale lips. "He is pink and plump. Couldn't wish for more."

Grandma Louise came and touched Mama's forehead. "We're here now, Marjorie."

Mama's chest rose, and her exhaled breath rattled in her throat. Her eyes never left Zillia's face. "You'll do fine. Just fine. Don't . . ." She gasped once more, and her eyes closed.

Zillia had to lean forward to catch the words.

"Don't tell Jeb about the trunk."

"Mama?" Zillia grabbed the hand once more, but the strength had already left her mother's fingers. She tugged at her mother's arm, but it dropped back, limp on the quilt.

A tear trickled down Grandma Louise's wrinkled cheek. "Go on to the kitchen, Zillia. The baby should be nearer to the fire with this night air comin' on. Soonie and I will clean up in here."

"I don't want to leave her," Zillia protested. But one glance at her mother's face and the world seemed to collapse around her, like the woodpile when she didn't stack it right.

How could Mama slip away? A few hours ago they'd been laughing while the hens chased a grasshopper through the yard. They'd never spent a night apart and now Mama had left for another world all together. She pulled her hand back and stood to her feet. She blinked, wondering what had caused her to make such a motion.

Soonie held the baby out. His eyes, squinted shut from crying, opened for a moment and she caught a hint of blue. Blue like Mama's.

Zillia took him in her arms. Her half-brother was heavier than he looked, and so warm. She tucked the cloth more tightly around him while he squirmed to get free. "I have to give him a bath." Red fingerprints dotted the blanket. "I need to wash my hands."

"Of course you do. Let's go see if the water is heated and we'll get you both cleaned up." Tears brimmed in Soonie's eyes and her lip trembled, but she picked the bundle of cloths that Grandma Louise had gathered and led the way into the kitchen, her smooth, black braid swinging to her waist as she walked.

Zillia cradled the baby in one arm, and her other hand strayed to her tangled mess of hair that had started the day as a tidy bun with ringlets in the front. What would Mama say? She stopped short while Soonie checked the water and searched for a washtub. *Mama will never say anything. Ever again.*

The baby began to wail again, louder this time, and her gulping sobs fell down to meet his.

Zillia sank to the floor, where she and the baby cried together until the bath had been prepared.

As Soonie wrapped the clean baby in a fresh blanket, Jeb burst into the house. He leaned against the door. "The doctor is on his way." His eyes widened when he saw the baby. "That's it, then? Boy or girl?"

"Boy." Soonie rose to her feet. "Jeb, where have you been? I saw you send someone else across on the ferry."

Jeb licked his lips and stared down at the floor. "Well, ah, I got word to the doctor. I felt a little thirsty, thought I'd celebrate. I mean, birthing is women's work, right?"

The bedroom door creaked open, and Grandma Louise stepped into the kitchen. Strands of gray hair had escaped her simple arrangement. Her eyes sparked in a way Zillia had only witnessed a few times, and shouldn't be taken lightly.

"Your thirst has cost you dearly, Jeb Bowen." Grandma Louise's Swedish accent grew heavier, as it always did with strong emotion. "While you drank the Devil's brew, your wife bled out her last hours. You could have spared a moment to bid her farewell. After all, she died to bring your child into the world."

Jeb stepped closer to Grandma Louise, and his lips twitched. Zillia knew he fought to hold back the spew of foul words she and her mother had been subjected to many times. Whether from shock or some distant respect for the elderly woman, he managed to keep silent while he pushed past Grandma Louise and into the bedroom.

Zillia stepped in behind him. Somehow, in the last quarter of an hour, Grandma Louise had managed to scrub away the worst of the blood and dispose of the stained sheets and petticoats. The blue quilt was smoothed over her mother's body, almost to her chin. Her hands where folded over her chest, like she always held them in church during prayer.

Tears threatened to spill out, but Zillia held them back. She wouldn't cry in front of Jeb.

The man reached over and touched Mama's cheek, smoothing a golden curl back into place above her forehead. "You was a good woman, Marjorie," he muttered.

"Jeb." Zillia stretched out her hand, but she didn't dare to touch him.

When he turned, his jaws were slack, and his eyes had lost their normal fire. "You stupid girl. Couldn't even save her."

Zillia flinched. A blow would have been better. *Surely the man isn't completely addled. Not even the doctor could have helped Mama.* She shrank back against the wall, and swallowed words dangerous to her own self.

Jeb stared at her for another moment, then bowed his head. "I guess that's that." He turned on his boot and walked out of the room.

2

River Lullaby

The late July sun hid its face the morning they laid Mama's body
to rest. Jeb stood alone by the head of the grave, staring at the sky
like he thought it would fall down and swallow him up. He
clutched a battered New Testament given to him by Pastor Fowler,
since he'd left the family Bible at home. When the pastor nodded
to him to read his verse, Jeb shook his head and stared down at the
plain wooden coffin sunk deep into the grave. His eyes matched
the dark hollow in the earth, and his shoulders trembled within the
old suit that had once belonged to Zillia's papa.

Zillia would have felt sorry for the man if she hadn't seen him
bully her mother throughout the last two years. Mama never made
excuses, only said, "don't ever let a man treat you like that, Zillia."

Her heart would have broken in two if she had known about the slap.

Then why did you let him hurt you? Zillia leaned forward to gaze at the coffin. Jeb had come into their lives a few months after Papa passed, a handsome stranger, brash and full of promises. Mama had been so lonely, so scared to be on the farm without a man's help and protection. *Any other man would have been better.*

The baby, still without a name, stirred in Zillia's arms. She hoped to goodness he stayed quiet for the service.

Almost everyone in the town came to the funeral. They sang the somber, beautiful hymns warbled at every funeral, about the 'sweet by and by' and the chariot swinging low. Zillia hadn't seen any chariots. What good was it for Mama to be so far away, even if she was on some 'beautiful shore?' She needed her here and now, to help care for the infant and tell her what to do. Her face burned with unshed tears. If she allowed herself to cry again, she might not be able to stop. So she focused on the blurred faces surrounding the grave.

Grandma Louise and Grandpa Walt were there, of course, singing through their tears. They loved Mama too, though she wasn't kin. Soonie and her brother, Wylder held the hands of their two cousins who had also been adopted by Grandpa and Grandma.

Wylder shifted and stared down at his feet. Zillia hadn't talked to him since before the birth, and she longed to hear his reassuring voice. Next to Soonie, he was her best friend and confidant. He glanced her way, and one corner of his mouth turned up between his carefully trimmed mustache and goatee. How she longed to be cozy and safe by the Eckhart's fire, surrounded by laughter and song instead of darkness and death.

Jeb's family stood across from her. Jemima Trent, Jeb's sister, didn't bow her head during prayer. Glittery eyes watched Zillia and the baby under her thick bangs and black netted veil. Her four sons, referred to as 'them Trent boys' even though everyone had passed eighteen, were subdued from their normal unruliness, with battered hats held in meaty hands. Their uncharacteristic reverence could only be due to the presence of their mother and Pastor Fowler.

Abel Trent, the youngest of the brothers, gave Soonie a wink.

Zillia gasped and glanced around to see if anyone else had noticed. *Could you go to hell for winking at a funeral?* On the other hand, Abel probably didn't think he had much to lose, with far worse trespasses on his record with the Almighty. *But he could have some respect for his own aunt.* She gave him an indignant glare.

He stared up at the sky, like he didn't notice.

The service closed while friends and family members dropped in handfuls of dirt and paid their last respects.

Zillia stepped out of the line to watch from the side. *I can't do it. Mama hated dirt.*

The pastor's wife, a tall woman with flaming red hair, came to where she stood and patted her hand with a wordless smile.

When the service finally ended, Pastor Fowler came over to shake Jeb's hand. "We are very sorry for your loss. Please let us know if we can help."

"We'll get by, Pastor." Jeb stood up straight and looked him in the eye. As pathetic as Jeb was, he had a proud streak and hated when other folks thought badly of him. No one, except Soonie's family to a small extent, knew his true nature.

The thought of residing in the same house with the man-made Zillia positively ill. But where else could she go? She couldn't leave the baby with only his father to care for him. A shudder ran across her thin shoulder blades.

People began move away from the gravesite. Zillia tucked her shawl around her sleeping brother and hurried towards the wagon. A brush of skirts followed her, and she turned to face Jemima Trent. The woman's smile was pinched, as though her face was unused to the expression.

"You poor dear." A claw-like hand clutched at Zillia's arm. "Having to mind that baby all by yourself! How are you managing?"

Zillia's first instinct was to step back out of the woman's reach, but she stood firm. "I... we're all right. Mama was only a few years older than me when I was born. If she managed, then so can I."

Jeb moved over to stand beside her. "Hello, Jemima. What do you think of the little runt?"

Without asking, Mrs. Trent yanked the baby from Zillia's arms. He opened his eyes, stared at her, and began to wail.

"He's a goodly one," Mrs. Trent yelled over the screams. "Not all puffy and red like some of them babies. I always wanted another child, after Samuel died. We have plenty of room, Jeb, I could care for the lad and raise him up right."

Jeb's eyebrows sank together over his beak-like nose. "Hmmm... I'll give it some thought. Might be for the best."

Memories rasped into Zillia's mind. Abel Trent coming into school, time and again, with bruises and black eyes. He'd always have an excuse. Some beatings came from his brothers, but she'd seen Mrs. Trent's temper in action. Her sons had been subjected to more than just venomous words. Zillia snatched her brother back.

Mrs. Trent's eyes popped open. "Well, I never!"

"You won't get him!" Zillia wrapped the baby back up in her shawl. "He's mine, from my mother, and he will never be yours! I'll be cold and in my own grave before you take him!"

The folks who still remained turned to see what was going on.

Grandma Louise was by her side in an instant, patting her shoulder. "Calm down, no one's taking the baby," she soothed.

Jeb stared at Zillia for a moment and his scowl deepened. "Fool women," he muttered.

"But... Jeb..." Mrs. Trent held out her hands.

"If she wants to stay up a few nights with that squalling child, let her," Jeb growled. "She'll get tired of it soon enough." He walked off in the direction of the saloon.

Zillia's heart beat under the baby's tiny head, while he squirmed to be free from his blanket. Why hadn't Jeb made her give the infant to his sister? Could it be he actually cared for his son and wanted him close by? She frowned. She'd never seen Jeb make a decision to benefit anyone but himself.

The next few days were a blur of smells and sounds. Soured milk, the baby's soiled clothing, and Zillia's own unwashed body and hair. Constant cries filled her ears and mind. Silence became a novelty.

On the third night, Jeb stormed into the kitchen while Zillia tried to calm the screaming child.

"Can't you make him shut up?" Sweat stained Jeb's long underwear. Scars created uneven patches in his graying beard.

The baby gave him a slanted look and cried louder.

"I don't know how to make him stop." *What would Mama have done to calm him down? Maybe just being his mother would have made a difference.* Zillia craned her neck to check the ornately carved clock on the mantelpiece. *2:30 am.* The baby had been fussing for over an hour. More than once, she had nodded off and woken up again with the baby in her arms, still crying with no indication he would ever stop. Plenty of chores awaited her in the morning. Jeb had yet to hold his child for one single minute.

Grandma Louise had given her a hasty tutorial on diaper changing and fixed up a bottle normally used for orphaned goats. Zillia had been worried about giving her brother goat's milk. "Won't that upset his stomach?"

Soonie had shrugged. "My cousin lived on horse's milk after my aunt passed away. And he hasn't been sick a day in his life!"

There had been little choice. No woman for miles had given birth recently to be a wet nurse. So far, the baby seemed to be doing fine with his alternative diet. At first Zillia had to dip her fingers in the warmed goat's milk for the baby to suckle, but he soon learned the bottle would bring better results.

Mama had spent months sewing garments for the child. If Zillia kept up with the washing he would be clothed. Grandma Louise promised to help shop for more supplies soon.

For two days after the funeral, women from town streamed in with condolences and baked goods. Most of the ladies came with pure motives, but some were ready to pounce on any juicy tidbit of information to take to town and pass around. People were hard up for gossip, and Mama's death and the poor baby left behind would be news enough to last all week, at least.

Jemima Trent had plunked her meat pie on the table and proceeded to inspect the house from corner to corner, all the while giving the baby greedy looks.

Zillia gave one syllable answers to their questions, and mostly just stood to the side, rocking the baby's cradle with her foot when he'd allowed her to put him down. She was thankful when the afternoons waned and the women would give up and go home to tend to their own families. After Jeb had eaten his fill, the rest of the food went to the chickens. Zillia couldn't swallow a bite.

These thoughts were interrupted by Jeb's scowl. "Are you even listening to me?"

An uneaten apple pie sat on the table at eye-level, and Zillia pictured herself hurling it into Jeb's face, the bits of crust and fruit sliding down over his neck. A tiny smile escaped her lips.

Jeb folded his arms and glared at her. "So you think it's funny now, huh? Look, if Little Jeb won't keep quiet, take him outside. I gotta sleep. This is making me crazy."

"Outside? What about coyotes? And snakes?" Zillia never went out after dark, and anyone who ventured in the night needed a gun. Wild pigs and cougars, which could be more dangerous than coyotes, had also been spotted in the area.

"Nothing's going to come near that squalling!" Jeb slammed the bedroom door.

He doesn't care if we live or die. If only Papa were here. He'd have never let us be treated like this. And Mama...

Warmth drained from her face and she had to convince her numbed arms to hold, hold on to her brother. She slumped into the rocker and gathered him close, despite his wails.

A banging came from the wall. *If he comes back out, he might hurt me again.* Her hand crept to her bruised face.

Zillia managed to stand. A quilt from the back of the rocking chair, wrapped around her shoulders, served for a shawl. She stepped into the summer night; the baby nestled in her arms.

The cricket's song swelled with the sound of the river, a constant rush below the line of trees and the twenty-foot bluff that kept the farm from floods. She had missed seeing the light dance on the water after three days of being cooped up inside. How could the crickets sing such a happy melody when the rest of the world seemed so wrong?

She sang to her brother, and gradually he quieted, his big eyes shiny with starlight, and a serious, very non-baby look on his face.

"Hush-a-bye,
Don't you cry,
Go to sleepy, little baby."

How cozy she used to feel as a little girl, in her Virginia nursery with its pink-papered walls and little canopied bed. Mama would sing to her even after she was far too old for lullabies. After Papa died two years ago, her mother started singing all the old songs again, and the melodies had comforted them both. Maybe tonight Zillia sang it as much for herself as for the little one, now asleep in her arms.

"When you wake,
You shall have

All the pretty little horses"

A peace settled over the closed eyes and perfect cheeks. His small white fingers with tiny slivers of nail curled tightly around her hand. Zillia bent down and kissed his forehead.

Years ago, Mama had taught her the constellations, both winter and summer. Zillia's favorite pattern, the mighty hunter, wouldn't be visible for several months yet. She missed him.

"You are mine, far more than you will ever be Jeb's," she whispered fiercely. "He won't be naming you after his nasty old self. I'm calling you Orion."

Her half-brother smiled in his sleep, as though he approved.

The mournful cry of a whippoorwill warbled though the pines. Zillia stroked Orion's impossibly soft curls and nodded. Only the whippoorwill had it right.

3

Miserable Morning

A tiny presence generated its own heat and added warmth to the bed. Zillia stirred, and the other body moved in response. She picked up the quilt that covered them. Little Orrie was cuddled beside her in her feather top bed, his chest rising and falling in a peaceful cadence.

She slipped the covers back and eased out of the bed, trying not to disturb his slumber; then placed pillows around him just in case. *Can a week-old infant roll over?* Soonie's cousins were the only children she had spent any time around and they had come to live with Grandma Louise when they were two and five. When she'd held infants in the past, they seemed so fragile in her clumsy hands. She had quickly passed them on to someone more competent.

After an attempt to move the heavy cradle up the ladder to her attic bedroom, she had given up and tucked Orrie in beside her. At first she worried about rolling over on him, but somehow she sensed his position, even when she was asleep. He woke fewer times in the night than when he slept by himself. She liked having him close, it seemed safer.

Her fingers fumbled to pull her thick, curly hair up and back for a new day. Boards creaked under her feet while she stumbled to the small washbasin and splashed lukewarm water on her cheeks. She paused for a moment at the reflection in the oval mirror that hung above the bowl. Could that really be her face? The week of sleepless nights had produced thick bags under her eyes, like dark beetles, waiting to jump out.

Mama would have helped her fix her hair and dabbed cream on her skin. "A ladies' complexion is of great importance," she would have said. Mama had been blessed with flaxen hair that always stayed where it was supposed to, and a face like the angels on the colored plates of the family Bible. Zillia had been given Papa's brown locks and skin prone to freckle, much to her despair.

Better get the fire stirred up and water boiling. Orrie will be up and crying for his milk. She sighed. She'd have to milk the goats first.

Chores tussled in her mind for attention. So many things had to be done just to keep everyone alive. Should she risk a slap and beg Jeb to do the milking today?

The ladder rungs seemed harder to descend this morning. She slipped down the last few and shuffled over to the stove.

Empty space met her hand when she reached under the table for the large kettle. *Funny. I know I put it there last night.* She rubbed her eyes and scanned the room. Only bare spaces met her gaze, instead of the items that had been in the same places for years. The clock. Her own china music box with the milkmaid. The set of brass fire tools. All the dishes in the pie safe. Gone.

A quick survey of Mama's room confirmed her fears. The spare sheets and quilt, ones not ruined during the birth, had been stripped from the bed, along with the feather top. Her mother's jewelry and trinkets, including the garnet ring that was to be Zillia's someday.

Anything of value that could be moved by one person, gone.

"Jeb!"

Orrie's thin cries drifted down the loft ladder, but she ignored them and ran outside in her nightgown. Dawn streamed into the farmyard.

The buckboard wagon her parents had purchased their first week in Texas was missing. The small thresher, and many of the farm implements. Anything that could fit into the wagon. Gone.

She rushed to the stables. Romulus and Remus, the beautiful matched team, had disappeared from their stalls, along with Eli, Jeb's riding stallion.

Sometimes, the mule, made a snorting noise in his corner.

"How could he leave us, Sometimes? Where did he go?" Orrie's last feeding had been at 3 am, which meant Jeb could have been gone for hours. *How did that clumsy man pack up the house and leave without waking me up?*

Her first instinct was to climb on Sometimes and gallop into town to send the sheriff after Jeb. But the man had a million excuses up his sleeve, he'd probably think of an explanation. The items did belong to his dead wife and he had a legal claim to them. And she couldn't leave Orrie by himself. She kicked the goat bucket and stood for a moment, breathing heavily, as it rattled down the hill and hit the side of the feeding trough.

Goats bleated from the yard, their swollen teats almost brushing the ground.

Zillia hurried into the house and climbed the ladder. Orrie stared up at her, eyes glassy with tears. His body heaved with sobs.

"I'm sorry, dear. I know you're hungry." She gathered him into a sling she'd fashioned from an old apron. He nuzzled against her shoulder while she climbed back down the ladder.

The water jug under the table was still there. She poured some into his bottle. "This will have to do until I finish the milking."

A thought hit her as Orrie pulled greedy draughts from the bottle. She scaled the ladder once more. In a dark corner of her room Mama's old trunk lay hidden under a pile of quilts. Once Mama realized the mistake she'd made by taking those vows before God and the church with that foul man, she made Zillia promise to never tell Jeb about it.

Zillia opened the chest. It contained some of Mama's dresses, too nice for every day or really most days in Bastrop. There were clothes Zillia had outgrown, saved just in case Mama had another little girl. "Which you aren't," she said to Orrie. Watercolor postcards with lacy borders from the relatives East, all dated from many years ago. Papa's century old rifle, which needed cleaning but worked just fine. Under everything else she found it; a small bundle wrapped in burlap.

"It's still here." Clasping it to her chest, she let out a deep breath. "We'll be all right for a little while, Orrie."

She tucked the bundle into her apron pocket and went back downstairs. The chickens had flapped over to join the goats in their ruckus, deafening even from the house. "I'm coming!" she yelled.

Sun blazed over the fields and the air shimmered over waves of grass before she finally began the fifteen-minute walk to Soonie's house with Orrie bundled up in her arms.

Wylder was repairing a wagon wheel in the yard when she approached the Eckhart's log cabin. He hoisted the giant sledgehammer above his head as though it were a toy, slamming it into the wooden peg that held the wheel secure. His blue eyes shone brighter when he turned and saw her.

Zillia realized she'd been staring and her cheeks grew warm. She studied her bare toes in the dirt. "He's gone."

"Jeb? Where'd he go?" Wylder leaned the hammer against the wagon and wiped sweat off his forehead.

"I don't know." Tears trickled down her cheeks and, to her dismay, over the bridge of her nose. The flour she had dusted over her freckles would be washed away.

Wylder stepped closer. "I'm sure he's just out drinking. He'll be back."

"He took almost everything," she sniffled and tried to stand up straighter.

"That no good …" Wylder's face darkened. "Well, I'm not going to say what I think." He turned away and stared out at the barn yard.

"I'm sorry, I didn't mean to cry. Is your grandma here, or Soonie?"

Soonie stepped outside the cabin door and into the yard. "Zillia, what brings you by? Why are you crying?"

"Jeb cut out," Wylder explained before she could reply.

Soonie said a word in Comanche that didn't sound ladylike. "No good evil man!" She stomped her bare foot on the dirt and opened the door again. "Grandma! Zillia's here!"

Grandma Louise bustled outside. She took one look at Zillia and ushered her into the kitchen. "Come on in, let's hear about it."

Zillia was directed to a rough, wooden bench and handed a cup of cold water.

Soonie took charge of Orrie. She fussed over him and kissed his chubby cheeks. "Oh, you get more handsome every day, Tahnee."

"What does that mean?" Zillia asked.

"Little one."

Soonie's mother had been half Comanche and had grown up on a reservation. Soonie embraced the ways of her mother's people. She wore buckskin clothing every day except for Sundays, and moccasins instead of store-bought shoes. Sometimes Zillia would see Soonie on her pony streaking across their field, hair whipping behind her like a living thing.

Grandpa Walt came in from the back room. He folded his thin, tall body into a wooden chair and nodded in Zillia's direction. "So Jeb headed for the hills?"

"Yes, sir," replied Zillia, managing to gulp back her tears this time.

"Your ma's family know she died and left you and the little baby?"

Zillia shook her head. "None of them approved when she married Jeb and no one has written since the wedding, not even to me. I never wanted Mama to marry Jeb. I didn't like him either."

Grandpa Walt's kind blue eyes studied her face. "They'll take you in, if you tell them what happened. They couldn't turn their backs on family."

If only he knew. After Mama had written her family to tell them of her sudden marriage, only one letter had come back. A cold, hateful letter. Her parents had both come from proud, affluent families and Mama's relatives could not accept that she'd married a stranger without consulting them. Zillia folded her arms. As much as she loved Grandpa Walt, she wouldn't be speaking of family business to anyone else.

Grandma Louise stopped by to stroke Orrie's downy hair. "Zillia, you're sixteen years old. You're a good, strong girl, but you can't be expected to care for this little baby and the farm all by your lonesome self. You have the goats, chickens, vegetable garden, the corn crop, horses..."

"Just the mule," Zillia said softly. "No horses anymore."

Grandpa Walt clutched his few remaining tufts of hair. "I'm not a swearing man, but by golly, what a monster!"

Zillia pulled out the burlap package. "He didn't take everything. That's one reason I came today." The rough cloth fell open to reveal six silver spoons and a golden brooch. "Could you sell these for me? I think they'd fetch enough to pay the harvest crew this fall, and have some money left over for food and other needs. I would take them into town myself, but I don't want anyone to know about this."

Grandma Louise dropped a kettle on the floor, and water splattered the room. "Look what you made me do, you and your crazy talk! You cannot live out there all on your own! You will come stay here, with us." She bent to wipe up the water with her apron. "Besides," she said between swipes, "Your family in Virginia will send for you when they find out what happened."

"If I don't stay on the land, some squatter will come along and claim it for themselves, you know that. And your house is full with little Will and Henry." Zillia knelt to help sop up the water with a cloth from the table. "I'll be eighteen in less than two years, of age to put my name on the deed. Only my mother's name is on it now, Jeb never went to the bank to have it changed." She froze. *Where was the deed? Did Jeb take it?*

"Bet he's regretting that," Grandpa Walt muttered.

"He's a proud man, but so lazy." Grandma Louise shook her head. "Probably thought he had all the time in the world."

"I will write my Grandma Rose." Zillia wrung the towel out in a washtub. "But for now, please don't tell anyone in town Jeb's gone." A sickening thought hit her. "Really, he could come back at any time."

Grandpa Walt shook his head. "That man? I bet he was drunk last night. Might of took everything without even thinkin'. Once he realizes what he's done, he won't be showin' his face in these parts, not if everyone's lookin' down on him."

Grandma Louise nodded. "I think that's why he didn't give the baby over to Jemima. He didn't want people to wonder why he couldn't care for his own child."

Wylder came in the house. He smelled like soap and his arms glistened with water droplets.

"Zillia is asking us not to spread Jeb's disappearance around town just yet," Grandpa Walt said to Wylder.

"The man should be shot." Wylder's voice had a dangerous edge to it. He went over to the fire and jabbed at the coals with a stick.

Little Will, Soonie's cousin, played with one of the brightly painted Swedish horses that usually graced the mantelpiece. Henry, the older cousin, came over to see Orrie. "Why does he smell so funny?" he asked Soonie.

Soonie sniffed his head. "Why do you smell so funny?" She looked over at Zillia. "I think it's time for someone's bath."

"No baths!" The little boy ran out of the room.

"Zillia's going to need some extra help around the farm." Grandpa Walt nodded towards Wylder. "I was thinking you and Soonie could give her a hand for a few hours here and there."

"Of course!" Soonie beamed. "I love the goats."

"I... I can pay you." Zillia sat back down and picked up her bundle. "I don't want to be beholden to anyone."

"Nonsense." Grandpa Walt took the broach and held it up to the light. "Your pa helped with the big barn three years ago after the fire and never asked for a penny. Your ma and pa always came to our aid when we needed them. Neighbors help each other out. Besides," he gazed at her from under bushy white eyebrows. "You'll only be here until your family writes. Then you and Orrie will be heading East."

"East?" Wylder's eyes narrowed.

"We'll see." Zillia lifted her chin. The letter to Virginia would never be sent.

THE RIVER GIRL'S SONG

OCTOBER 1886

4

Sunday

The edge of the wooden pew pressed through the thin fabric of Zillia's summer dress. Sweat trickled down her brow, soaking her sunbonnet's brim. Ladies' hats bobbed up at the beginning of each hymn, then sank down with the solemn "Aaamennn."

Zillia's fingers trembled around the worn cover of the Methodist Hymnal. When she tried to read the tiny type, her eyes blurred. Orrie still hadn't decided to adopt normal sleeping patterns, and she'd had no time for breakfast before church.

Music swelled through the small but ornate sanctuary, over the pews and altar and up to the two stained-glass windows donated by the mayor. Zillia tilted her head to see the carefully cut dove, frozen in flight for eternity, about to settle on the head of Christ after He was baptized. Could God hear their song? Surely He stepped a bit closer to Earth to listen when His people sang.

The old-fashioned words sounded beautiful and mysterious, but she rarely understood them. Should she sing to God when she didn't know what she was saying?

She shrugged. They wouldn't allow those songs in church if God didn't like them.

Pastor Fowler stepped up to the pulpit. After the last strains of music died away, he beamed at the organist. "Miss Annette, you did a lovely job today. Thank you."

The lady turned as pink as her organza dress and floated down the aisle to her seat, where she settled down like a content chicken.

The Methodist tradition was to switch out the pastor every few years. Pastor Fowler had only been in the position for a couple of months. So far, the town seemed to accept the new man of the cloth, though sometimes he scandalized folks with scriptures no pastor had spoken in The Bastrop First Methodist Church sanctuary. Last week's sermon about fallen angels coming to earth to produce giants had been especially unusual. But folks couldn't deny the words from their very own Bibles, so most resigned themselves to learn the new thoughts. Soonie and Zillia would sit forward in their pew to listen to the fresh ideas, and often discussed them after church.

Though Pastor Fowler's face was serious when he looked out on the congregation, his eyes twinkled. Despite a heavy application of grease, a few hairs still stuck up on his head like silvery blades of grass. He flipped through his Bible and adjusted his spectacles. "Today we will study Proverbs 14:34. 'He that opresseth the poor reproacheth his Maker: but he that honoureth him hath mercy on the poor.'"

He turned to another section. "I have also chosen for us to read 2 Corinthians 9:7."

The man paused while his congregation searched for the verse. When pages stopped flapping, he started to read again. "'Every man according as he purposeth in his heart, so let him give; not out of necessity: for God loveth a cheerful giver.'

"Two examples, from many I could have chosen, describe the importance of giving to the poor." Pastor Fowler looked over his Bible and caught Zillia's eye. "The poor will always be among us, and God wishes us to honor Him by honoring them."

Zillia fought the urge to scrunch down in her seat like a little girl. If she turned her head, she knew every eye in the church would be fixed on her.

Four months had passed since Jeb left. Mama had planned to sew two new dresses for Zillia after the baby was born, but the cloth hadn't even been purchased. Her skirts were inches too short, even after she let them out. Patches adorned her elbows, and her shoes threatened to split apart with each step. Every Sunday she fought her pride to walk out the door and go to church, where, years ago, she'd been the best-dressed girl in the congregation.

A few bundles had arrived from 'charitable' people in the town. Aprons stiff with food stains, and petticoats with holes too large to patch. Most ended up in the rag basket.

She laced her fingers together, forcing her hands into her lap to keep them from covering her face. Pastor Fowler probably hadn't meant to hurt her feelings. But this sermon would be sure to generate more 'helpful' bundles from people who would then go on their way, feeling righteous and generous.

If she ever found herself in a place of prosperity again, she'd give to those less fortunate. But they would never know the giver, and she'd only donate things worth giving.

Zillia glanced over at Soonie. Her friend's eyes shone, and she mouthed the words along with Pastor Fowler when he quoted a scripture. Soonie's happy smile melted into a look of confusion when she saw Zillia's face.

I must look like a thundercloud. Mama always said her thoughts wrote themselves into her expressions. After a moment's concentration, she managed to relax the muscles around her mouth and eyes in what she hoped would be a more pious look. *I don't need anyone thinking I've gone mad and can't care for Orrie.*

At least one person in town already thought she was an unfit caretaker. The second the pastor dismissed the congregation, Jemima Trent charged over to Zillia's pew, making high pitched noises at Orrie.

Zillia's stomach grew queasy like it always did at the sight of the stocky, pig-eyed woman. She smiled. *I'll do my best to avoid a scene in church.* "Hello, Mrs. Trent. How are you this morning?"

"How is my nephew?" Jemima jabbed a red finger at Orrie's cheek. "You look thin, poor little baby!" Her eyes narrowed at Zillia. "Sister's not feeding you enough, is she?"

Zillia choked back her anger and turned to keep Orrie out of the odious woman's reach. She spoke over her shoulder, not caring how rude it looked. "He's fine. The doctor said he's gaining weight like he should be. Goodness knows I give him plenty of goat's milk, and I've started him on cornmeal mush."

"Let me have my little nephew." Jemima tugged at Zillia's arm. "He needs to know what it's like to have a real mother hold him."

Zillia jerked away from her grasp. "Excuse me. I need to go now. Soonie will have the wagon pulled around and I don't want her to have to wait on me."

Jemima wrinkled her nose. "You spend far too much time with that injun family. My brother should have sent the baby to me afore he left on that business trip." She leaned close enough for Zillia to whiff the liver and onions she must have had for breakfast. "I'll bet he told you to bring him over, didn't he?"

"He did no such thing!" Zillia threaded her way through the pews towards the door.

Before she could move out of earshot, she heard Jemima Trent tell another woman, "Girl puts on all those Virginia airs, even though she comes to church dressed like a farm hand. Everyone knows that baby would be better off with me. Haven't I raised four boys already?"

Swift steps took Zillia outside before she could hear the other woman's reply.

Blessed day! Wylder had driven the wagon over, with Soonie, Grandma Louise and the two little boys already settled in. Grandpa Walt had stayed home with what he called 'ailments.' She handed Orrie to Soonie and swung up and in with everyone else.

The church door cracked open, and Jemima Trent waddled down the porch steps. Her mouth was open in some sort of screeching command.

"Drive, Wylder, please!" Zillia shouted.

Wylder clucked to the horses, and they lurched away.

Zillia's head ached, and her jaw hurt from clenching her teeth so hard. *Perhaps I should become Presbyterian. Then I wouldn't have to see that woman every week.*

Zillia threw two more handfuls of weeds on the growing pile outside the garden fence. The exposed roots filled the air with a rich, earthy scent. She bent down to pull a few more from around the vines of the late fall squash harvest, moving with care so she wouldn't disturb Orrie, who slept peacefully in the sling on her back.

Wylder came back from the edge of the field where he had just dumped a load of dirt clods too baked by the Texas sun to be worth the effort of breaking up. He peered under her sunbonnet. "You look tired. Are you all right?"

Zillia stared at him. She wanted to yell, "I'm sixteen and I've been up all night with a screaming child. I'm trying to prove to everyone I'm capable of running a farm. What do you think? Of course I'm not all right!"

Instead she remembered her mother. How she patiently stacked firewood and cooked bread, even when her ankles swelled and her back ached. How she'd bake her special treats and help her with lessons and oh, the hundreds of other things she did every day. No matter how exhausted and weary she must have felt, she never complained.

She forced a smile. "I'm fine. Thank you for asking."

The vegetable garden was small, and with help from Soonie and Wylder, could be tended in a few hours. The corn fields would pose a much bigger challenge. Every year since Papa's death, the harvest had been smaller, and this year, with Jeb at the helm, it had been halved. Jeb had spent up Mama's savings long before. Could she truly sow the fields and deal with the harvest in the years to come, even with the help of her friends?

When she squinted her eyes, she could almost see Papa, strong and proud, in the fancy suit he'd worn as a banker in Virginia. He had taken her out to the field the week they arrived in Bastrop, while workers were still building the house. Mama chose to stay in town at the hotel.

"What do you think, Zillia, my dove?" He had stretched out his arms. "All this land, not a neighbor in sight. We can be free out here. Free to do whatever we wish."

"But it's dirty, Papa." Though she had only been six, Mama was already dressing her in the latest fashions. "I'm getting dust on my shoes."

A grin had spread over his face. "Better get used to it, little one. Don't worry, you're going to love it here. Pretty soon you'll be jumping in haystacks and swimming in the river, just like I did on my grandparent's farm when I was a boy. Put some roses in those pale cheeks." He stooped down and kissed her.

"Those things aren't ladylike, Papa. Can we go back to town?"

Papa had taken her hand and pulled off the little white glove she had been wearing. He pressed something small and warm into her palm. "You know what that is, my dear?"

When Zillia opened her hand, she saw a shriveled, orange seed. Her first thought was to drop it on the ground, but she didn't want to hurt Papa's feelings. She examined it closer.

"Is this—corn, Papa?"

"That's right. And I want you to put it in the dirt, right here. You get to plant our first seed. It's a seed of dreams, Zillia. The dream I've had for years and years. I hope that after a little while, you will understand and love it too."

Despite her misgivings, she'd felt a tiny thrill when she poked a hole in the small mound of dirt, dropped in the seed, and covered it again. Because of her deed, life would come. Papa wanted it to happen, and she would have done anything in the world for him.

Squeaking wheels from down the road interrupted her memory. "Is Grandpa Walt back from town already?" she asked Soonie.

"Grandpa takes his time." Soonie shaded her eyes and stared out at the road. "Even if he didn't meet someone to talk to, he'd still have to examine all the new tools in the general store and tell Mr. Grayson why none of them are as good as the old ones."

"That's not our draft team." Wylder joined the girls. "Those are town horses."

A small buggy drawn by two black thoroughbreds appeared, confirming his words.

"Abel Trent," Wylder muttered. "Almost made it through the week without seeing his ugly face."

"What's he doing out here?" Zillia's chest tightened, like it always did when she saw a Trent boy. And Abel was the worst of them.

The Trent family had come to Bastrop three years ago. Though, like Wylder, Abel was two grades ahead of Zillia, all the students shared the same class. Abel was tall for his age, what Grandpa Walt called "Grown-man sized." He'd used this feature to his advantage and bullied his classmates, especially Soonie and Wylder.

When Jemima Trent had found out about Soonie and Wylder's heritage, she filed a complaint with the school board. Of course, it was dismissed immediately. The Eckharts were upstanding citizens. Soonie and Wylder never caused trouble.

Abel made a big show about sitting in the farthest desk from them as possible. He'd come in, pinch his nose and declare 'it smells like injun in here! Don't you ever take a bath?" though many times he brought in undesirable odors of his own. Abel was one reason Zillia hadn't felt bad about missing school when the fall term started.

The buggy sped towards them. Abel crouched over the reins as though he were watching for road bandits. He pulled the horses up short and their dusty hooves pawed the air. Blood and foam flecked their mouths around the metal bits.

"That boy ruins horses faster than anyone I've ever met," Wylder muttered as he set off toward the buggy. Zillia and Soonie glanced at each other and followed him.

Abel swung down from the seat, narrowly missing a kick from one of the steeds. He stumbled out of the way.

Since the Trent boys never came to church, Zillia hadn't seen Abel since the funeral. He seemed bigger and even more surly, if possible.

Abel raised a giant hand to his eyes and surveyed the farm without so much as a hello. His stare ended when he caught sight of Soonie. A wicked leer spread across his face.

"Can we help you, Mr. Trent?" Wylder's voice was molten steel as he stepped in front of his sister.

"Ah, the half-breeds." Abel's voice was a combination grunt and guffaw. "Don't got no business with you today, leastways, I don't think I do." He pointed at Zillia. "I need to speak with you, Cousin of sorts." His fingernail was black and crusted over with yellow fungus.

"I don't hold you as kin, you know that, Abel," Zillia crossed her arms. "I'd thank you to state your business and leave."

"Oh, I don't aim to stay." Abel put his hands on his hips. "I came to find out what's going on with my uncle."

Zillia stretched to her fullest height, which caused her to land right at Abel's shoulder. "Jeb found a trading partner in North Dakota and struck out on a new venture. He's pretty sure he'll come back with a wagon load of cash. I told your mother months ago." The lie had been concocted by Grandpa Walt, and it burned Zillia's tongue every time she told it. But if she hadn't found a way to explain Jeb's absence Orrie could be taken away. Abel gnashed his tobacco-stained teeth at her. "Yep, you told her all right. How come he didn't let us know he was going? After all, we're family. And why did I find this at the trading post across the river? Owner wouldn't tell me where he got it, but he gave it back after I made him." He opened his hand to reveal a small, silver object.

A pocket watch, unmistakably Jeb's since his initials were carved into the back. Jeb had taken the trinket, a wedding present from her mother, when he left. How had it ended up at the trading post?

"I don't know. Jeb might have needed money for his trip. Maybe he sold it on his way out." Zillia tried to speak evenly, but anger threatened to boil over. *Jeb has no shame, selling Mama's gift to him.*

"Know what I think?" Abel's eyes grew hard and glittery. "I think someone knocked him off."

It took a moment for Zillia to grasp his meaning. "You... you think someone killed Jeb?"

"Yep. And I think you know all about it."

Wylder snorted. "That's a pretty far-fetched idea, even for you, Mr. Trent."

"Yeah, you think? Mebbie it's not. Mebbie you did it, Mister Eckhart. You might just have my poor uncle's scalp tacked to your cabin wall. Mebbie my brothers and I should come over and find out."

"Get off my land." Zillia stomped her foot, and Orrie whimpered. "You're not welcome here. Go away and don't come back."

"That's almost an admission of guilt right there," Abel taunted.

Wylder gripped his hoe a little tighter. "You heard what she said."

Abel stepped back. "Yeah, well, I don't really feel safe here, anyways. No telling what you murdering savages will get into your heads." He climbed back into the seat and slapped the reins over the glossy black backs. The horses bolted and were a quarter of a mile down the road before Abel regained control.

"Man shouldn't be allowed to own horses." Soonie turned back to the garden. "Sun's almost gone. What a waste of daylight!"

Another wagon rattled down the road, this time Grandpa Walt with his buckboard. The elderly man stopped the cart and lumbered over the side. "Everything all right over here?"

Zillia told him about Abel's visit while they walked back to the house and washed up at the pump. "Do you think I should be worried?" she finished.

Grandpa Walt shook his head. "That man is all talk and bluster, like his whole family. Why don't we go in the house? I have something to show you."

Zillia lit the lanterns and stirred up the fire in the stove. Orrie started fussing for his bottle so she got it ready. Soonie ladled out the beans that had been cooking all day. Wylder brought in another armload of firewood. Grandpa Walt sat in Papa's chair, watching them contentedly. "Those vittles smell good."

Zillia sat in the rocking chair with Orrie. "All right, Grandpa Walt. What did you want me to see?"

"Well... I should have given you this sooner, but Soonie just told me you'd been looking for it." Grandpa Walt pulled a crumpled paper out of his pocket and handed it to her.

Zillia unfolded it with her free hand and glanced over the document. "This is Mama's signature!" she gasped. Sometimes Grandpa Walt's absentmindedness was exasperating.

"Yes. It's the deed to the land. Your mother gave it to me to keep safe."

Several times she had torn the house apart to look for the deed, and even checked at the bank to see if it had been stored in a lock-box there. It hadn't occurred to her to ask Grandpa Walt if he knew where it was. What a relief to hold it in her hand!

"I wonder why Mama didn't tell me about this?"

Soonie scraped up her last spoonful of beans from the tin plate. "I'm sure it was just for caution's sake, so Jeb couldn't make you tell."

The girls gathered dishes and stacked them by the counter washtub. Grandpa Walt stood, stretching his leathery arms into the air and almost snapping his overall straps. "We'd best be getting home. Don't want Grandma Louise to wonder what's become of us."

Wylder brought his bowl to Zillia and leaned over. "Come outside with me, Zillia, just for a few minutes."

"All right." She glanced over. Orrie was asleep in his cradle. "Soonie, can you mind Orrie for a moment?"

Soonie looked up from the dishes and nodded.

Zillia followed Wylder outside. The sun was gone, but the impossible colors of evening remained. Golds and pinks and deep reds stained the skies, bordering feathery clouds.

Wylder walked out to the fence and put his hands in his pockets. He let out a low whistle. "Sure is beautiful out here, isn't it?"

"Yes, I guess it is." Zillia poked at a rock with her toe.

He put his hands behind his head and leaned back against the fence. "Remember when we were little kids? We'd sit out here and pretend we could climb up the clouds."

Zillia smiled. "I thought if we could find a tree tall enough, maybe we could get to Heaven without having to die. Like the prophet Elijah."

Wylder turned and studied her. "You have to give yourself time to enjoy things. Like this sunset. If you worry too much, you'd miss it."

"Sure, Wylder. Today was a bit—unsettling."

His eyes narrowed. "I'm not going to let Abel Trent bother you."

"I know," Zillia said. Any member of the Eckhart family would fight to the death for her and Orrie, and she'd do the same for them, but it was nice to have Wylder come out and say it. "I just hated when he accused you of those terrible things. Especially when Jeb is so despicable."

Grandpa Walt walked up behind them. "Don't think you'll be bothered by any of the Trents for a while."

"What do you mean?" Zillia asked.

"Didn't I tell you? Mr. Bell, the ferry owner, heard from the sheriff. Jeb's gone and attempted a manslaughter. He'll be in jail for quite some time."

A wave of relief like Zillia hadn't felt in months flooded over her. She sagged back against the fence. "For how long?"

Grandpa Walt shrugged. "Don't know the particulars. But the Trent family has their pride. They won't be making much of a stir for a while. And I'm your official guardian until it's all sorted out. I've already smoothed over details with the sheriff. Normally he wouldn't allow it without written consent of a parent, but since we're good friends and all, he went ahead and approved the measure. One thing's for sure, I'd be surprised if Jeb ever shows his face in these parts again."

Zillia didn't share Grandpa Walt's conviction. But at least she had a bit of reprieve from the Trent family. Abel must not have heard the news, or he would never have ventured out with his bluster and accusations.

Later, Zillia watched while her friend's lanterns bobbed through the darkness to the wagon. She called goodbyes until everyone was too far away to hear. While she stepped in and bolted the door, she tried to ignore the knot in her stomach that cinched tighter every time she was left alone.

JULY 1887

5

Soap and a Savior

"Maaaaaa!" A goat begged for breakfast through the wooden fence. Her twins pressed tiny faces next to hers.

"Zilly, goats." Orrie's curls bobbed while he grabbed fistfuls of grass and held them out to the animals.

"Yes, goats." Zillia poured grain into a bucket and dumped the water pail to refill at the pump. *Thank God for the goats.* Her mother had purchased them the spring before her passing.

When Orrie had outgrown his bottle, Zillia began to sell milk to neighboring farms for a good price. It had taken a little convincing for some of her neighbors to make a switch, but they all agreed the goat's milk had a better flavor.

Green stalks of corn swayed in the summer breeze. Zillia had begun to prepare the land for her second crop months before, after the frost pulled back its chilly fingers from the earth. She had no high hopes for this year's harvest. But what else could she do? The land would soon be overcome with brush and weeds if she didn't clear it out. Zillia pressed on. She'd hitch Sometimes to the plow and trudge behind him for acres at a time. They'd move along for an hour or two, until Sometimes dug his hooves into the sand and refused to go any further.

She didn't pay attention to how much time slipped by, just worked through to make it until the next sunrise. And she managed to keep going, with the help of Soonie and Wylder. It was wrong to depend on them so much. But they brought warmth and friendship in the back of their wagon, along with borrowed tools and food from Grandma Louise. If they didn't come to help, she would have surely died from loneliness.

Grandpa Walt nagged her about the Virginia relatives until she finally told him she had written them and no one had replied. It seemed like the more lies she told, the easier it became, like each bite of Eve's apple.

What would Grandma Rose and Aunt Darlene say if they knew their granddaughter worked in the fields all day and shot vermin at night? Probably nothing. The last letter they had sent her mother had been filled with vicious words Zillia would never forget. Mama had been confused about Jeb, that was certain, but she hadn't deserved such hate.

Last week, Zillia and Orrie had celebrated his second birthday over a crumbly piece of johnny cake. The little boy learned new words and skills every day. At times she wondered if her brother was the most clever child in the world. Of course, she would never share this thought with Soonie.

Zillia filled the feeding pail on the milking stand and let the goats into the gate one at a time to have their breakfast and be milked. If only she could let go of the corn crop and focus on the goats! She leaned against the stand to rest. She couldn't lose the land Papa had worked so hard for, or the home he had designed and helped to build.

No spoon money remained, so she'd have to use proceeds from the corn to pay the harvest crew. Zillia had sold clothes, furniture and anything else in the home that could be spared.

Today she had a new project in mind. For the last two years she had purchased small cakes of soap from the dime store, wincing at the waste when she dropped coins in the shopkeeper's hand. Today she would try to make her own.

Soonie had scoffed at the notion. "You've never been to our house on soap day. It's a nasty, difficult process. Better just buy it from the store like your mama always did. It's harder to make than you think."

"Yes, but soap is expensive. I can make a big batch all at once and save money. Any penny saved is a good thing."

How satisfying it would be to open her wooden box and see smart, square bars of soap to supply them for months to come.

How hard could it be? *Surely, not as difficult as mucking a stall or plowing a field.*

Zillia left the goats and went to the darkest corner of the barn where she had stored containers of lye and lard. She opened the lye bucket and poked at the gray liquid with her feather. The quill dissolved in seconds. *Finally.* For weeks she had experimented to get the right consistency.

When she lifted the lid of the lard container, she covered her nose and tuned away with a gasp. How could something so rancid be used as a cleanser? No wonder Mama had never attempted to make her own. She slammed the lid down and hauled the bucket to the outside fire pit, then lugged out the lye pail. With grim determination, she lit the fire.

"Zilly, Zilly, come see." Orrie toddled from the side yard and tugged at her skirts. "Come see duckies."

"Orrie, I can't right now. I'm doing something important. Wait for a little while." She hung the heavy iron kettle over the fire and dumped in the bucket of lard.

"Ew." Orrie wrinkled his freckled nose. "What's that?"

"I'm... making soap." Zillia scooped dripping fat back into the pot with her wooden spoon. She squinted down at Grandma Louise's wobbly instructions. "Add lye a little at a time, then stir slowly." She peered into the kettle. "Hmmm. I think it needs to melt some more. What do you think, Orrie?"

Silence answered her. "Orrie?" She glanced to the side of the house, then around the goat shed. "Orrie, where did you go?"

55

Her brother's curls bobbed over the ridge, several hundred yards away. She ran after him and grabbed him by his overall strap. "Orrie, I'll take you down to the river after we make some soap, all right?" She pulled him back in the direction of her project.

"Duckie!" Orrie threw himself on the ground and drummed his bare feet against her shins, his sharp ankles digging through her skirts and petticoat.

"Ow! Stop that! I'll get your ark down and you can play in the yard."

"Ark?" The rage on Orrie's face mellowed into a sweet smile.

On the way to the house to fetch the toy, Zillia lifted the pot lid to check her soap. The fat had almost completely melted. *I should add the lye soon.*

Once inside the cabin, she pulled the Noah's ark down from its place on the mantelpiece. Wylder and Grandpa Walt had carved the pieces through the cold winter evenings and presented it to Orrie for his birthday. They had hollowed out an oak log, shaped it into a boat, and painted it in bright colors. From time to time they presented Orrie with a new pair of animals. So far he owned giraffes, bears, elephants, zebras, and of course, Noah.

She carried the ark into the yard and set it at a safe distance from the fire.

"Ark, Ark." Orrie crowed happily. He squatted down in the sand and lined the animals up in rows.

Zillia checked the fat. "Time to add the lye."

How much was a little at a time? The lye bucket slipped in her hands, and she splashed in a generous amount. *I hope that wasn't too much.* Stir it in. Pour in a little more.

"Duckies." Orrie's red face appeared next to the pot. His eyes scrunched into little slits, and tears streamed from the corners. Animals, ark and patriarch were scattered in the sand.

"Orrie, be careful. Grandpa Walt and Wylder spent a lot of time on those." Zillia dusted them off and scooped them back into the ark.

The stench of a very burnt something interrupted her chore. Dark slime bubbled over the sides of the pot and dripped into the fire.

"Oh no!" Zillia swung the heavy kettle over to the side and away from the heat. The lid slid off to reveal blackened chunks floating in a pool of ooze.

The lid fell out of her hands and she sat down hard on a stump. The noon sun beat down over the mess. *Half the day is gone. How?*

"Zilly!" Faint and far away.

"Orrie?" She leapt to her feet. "Orrie, where did you go?"

"Zilly!"

The river. The hem of Zillia's filthy skirts tangled around her feet and tripped her up while she ran down the bluff. "Orrie, I'm coming. Where are you?" She reached the edge of the river and pushed through tangles of vines and brush. Orrie's footprints dug deep into the sand, then disappeared into the water.

"Orrie!" she screamed.

"Zilly!"

Sticks and logs had gathered in the depths of the river over time and formed an island. Orrie's tiny face peeped out of the branches. He stood up and waved. "Zilly, duckies."

"How on earth?" *How could a two-year-old child reach the center of the river?* She ran along the bank, searching for a way across. A log jutted out to the island. Orrie must have crawled over, using it for a bridge. Murky water lapped and tugged at the pile of sticks. The river was unusually high and swift for this time of year.

What if Orrie had been swept away? She couldn't harbor such a terrible thought. *He's fine, I just have to figure out how to get him back on the shore.* The log was too shaky to hold her weight. Papa had taught her how to swim, but it had been years since she'd been in deep water.

A few steps in, and the water already reached her waist. River mud tugged at bare toes with each movement. *Closer.* The water lapped against her chest and the current pulled at her dress like witches' fingers. Why hadn't she taken off her clothes? Her brittle, cracked corset dug into her ribs.

Orrie grinned and held up a ball of yellow fluff. "Duckies!"

Indignant quacks came from the mother duck. She flapped her wings and swam in circles around the island.

Finally, Zillia reached the pile of sticks. She stretched out her arms but couldn't touch her brother. "Orrie, please come to me.

The ducks are in their nest, and we need to go to our house." She pointed to the mother duck. "See? She's scared of us. We should go away so she can take care of her babies."

Orrie frowned. "My ducky." He pulled the duckling close to his chest. The tiny bird opened and closed its bill and squirmed to get away.

"Come on, Orrie." If she tugged on the logs, she risked pulling the whole island apart. "You're going to hurt it. Maybe we can buy a little ducky next time we're in town. Would you like that?"

"My ducky." Orrie stomped a foot and almost lost his balance.

How can someone so cute be so much trouble? Zillia pulled herself closer and reached for Orrie's ankle. "You get over here right now!"

He scooted out of the way, laughing.

Her thoughts raced. What could she do? "I'll give you a peppermint stick," she promised.

Orrie's face lit up. "Okay, Zilly." He placed the duckling back into the nest, where it settled down among its siblings.

"All right, now come over here." Zillia tugged on his sleeve. She finally managed to pull him into the water.

"Cold, Zilly!" he squealed and struggled to get away.

Zillia fought to hold him in one arm while she moved back towards the shore. "Just a little way, then we'll go home and get dry clothes."

Halfway to the shore, her feet slipped. She screamed and scrambled but could not regain her hold on the slippery rocks. In an instant she and Orrie were swept into the current. Orrie somehow managed to hang on to her neck while she kicked and struggled toward another log.

Fingers slipped on the moss then held. Coughing and gasping, she clung to the wood and the little boy. Her toes felt for a surface, but this area was too deep for her to reach the bottom.

"Zilly, Zilly!" Orrie's tiny chin stuck out above the waves and he gasped for air.

"Hold on, Orrie," she cried. "Hold on to me."

"Help!" she called out, though it seemed a futile plea. "God, if you're listening, please help us!"

Her fingers were becoming numb as the current tugged on them. Orrie's hands gripped her neck so tight she thought he'd choke the life out of her.

What if she was being punished for lying? *But Orrie didn't do anything wrong.* "God, I'm sorry. Please help us. Please!"

"Zillia!" a faint voice floated from the bank. "Zillia, I'm here! I'm coming down!"

She turned her head just enough to see Wylder burst through the trees along the riverbank. He pulled out a long section of thick, rope-like grapevine. His knife glinted in the sun and the vine snaked out on the ground.

"Grab this!" He threw it out to her.

With what hand? "Orrie, you have to hug me tighter."

Orrie's grip tightened as Zillia let go of the log. Her scrambling fingers reached for the vine, which had floated beside her, and she caught it. *There!* She wrapped the thick vine around her arm.

Wylder tugged on the other side, and peace and security flooded through her soul. Only a few yards over, and once more Zillia's feet dug into the mud. The vine slid from her fingers, and she scooped Orrie into her arms.

Wylder waded in to help them to shore.

What a blessed relief to feel the powdery sand beneath her toes. Zillia sank to the ground. "Thank you, God," she whispered over and over, hugging Orrie close.

Her brother squirmed and tried to get away. "Zilly's wet."

Wylder laughed. "You'll be fine. In this heat both of you will be dry before we get to the house." He pried Orrie from Zillia's arms and held his hand out to her.

"Thank you." Her shaking fingers closed around his wrist and she pulled up to stand.

He pulled her close and let her lean on him on the way up the hill.

The sun shone, and goats bleated as though nothing had happened, as though she hadn't almost lost her little brother. A sob caught in her throat and she gulped it back.

Once home, they rushed to get Orrie into dry clothes. He seemed fine despite the ordeal and fell asleep clutching one of his painted zebras.

Zillia changed into a clean dress and came down to sit beside Wylder, who was poking up the coals in the stove.

"Better stay here for a while. Even though it's a hot day you don't want to catch a cold." He looked her over as though checking for signs of impending pneumonia.

Obediently, she scooted closer on the bench and held out her hands. "How could I have been so stupid? I almost lost him today, Wylder."

He put down the poker and rested his chin on his folded hands. "You would have thought of something. Neither one of you were hurt, that's what counts."

"No." Zillia shook her head. "Today shouldn't have happened. It wouldn't have happened to Mama. Maybe I've been wrong to try this. Orrie needs a home with two parents who will take better care of him." Just speaking the words made her shiver.

Wylder grasped her cold shoulder with his warm hand and gently pulled her around to face him. "Zillia, you can't believe that. You've done a wonderful job. Better than most girls could, that's for sure. Every baby gets into trouble sometimes. Grandma Louise will tell you. I almost burnt the house down when I was three."

"Really?"

Wylder nodded. "It's just by the grace of God Almighty any of us live until tomorrow." He leaned closer, until their foreheads almost touched. "You're doing the best you can, and it amazes me every day."

Warmth finally flowed into her, and as her spirit thawed, she began to cry again.

Wylder touched a tear with his finger. "No need for those."

Is he going to kiss me? He had done it once. Four years ago, when in the woods with Soonie on a picnic. Zillia had tripped over a log and twisted her ankle. She'd started crying, and he just bent down and kissed her, right on the lips. Carried her all the way home, too. He'd never mentioned it afterwards, and she decided he'd just wanted to help her feel better.

Would I want him to kiss me again? Maybe. She stayed perfectly still.

He drew back and folded his hands. "I have to head home. We're cleaning the barn out today. Will you be all right until Soonie can check on you this evening?"

Zillia released the breath she'd been holding and nodded. "Thank you, Wylder. Not just for saving our lives today, but for everything."

"Any time." He rose, tipped his hat, and walked out the door.

OCTOBER1888

6

Grove Harvest

Corn kernels flowed through Zillia's hands while she measured them into barrels. Two full bushels left for seed. Even after a hailstorm and not enough rain, she hadn't thought it would be this bad. Her shoulders slumped. No point in trying to grow enough to sell next year. If she was lucky they'd be able to feed the goats and themselves after the next harvest. Papa had never cried in front of her, but if he saw the state of his farm he would shed bitter tears.

Fields of stubble stretched before her. It had seemed like so much. But after twelve years of farm life, she knew better.

After they loaded the corn into his wagons last evening, the buyer had counted a few limp dollars into her hand. "Sorry, Miss.

Prices are down again this year."

The bills had crinkled as Zillia clenched her fist and stuffed them into her apron pocket. "Thank you, Mr. Brett." The money would pay the two hired harvesters and the rental of the thresher machine, that would be all.

Canned vegetables, fruit preserves and dried meat they had in plenty. Winter clothes for Orrie and herself, along with staples such as sugar and flour, would have to be paid for with egg and milk money or they'd just have to do without.

Why can't I have one easy day? Zillia slid down next to the corn barrels. Pastor Fowler always said ingratitude to the Almighty was the worst of sins. Sometimes she grew weary of spending all her functions trying to figure things out.

Memories of Virginia taunted her. Her sixth birthday party with six little girls, cake and lemonade. Winter, with sleigh-riding parties in the powdery drifts of snow. She'd learned to ice skate right before her parents brought her to Texas. She shook her head. They'd never have ice like that here in Bastrop.

She slapped on the tops of the corn barrels and tacked them down with a few nails. The containers went into the barn to save for next year, if the rats didn't get into them. "And I just bet they will," she whispered fiercely.

Once outside, she eyed the pile of firewood by the side of the house. She'd have to start chopping a small amount each day. While Texas winters rarely brought snow, they did possess many freezing nights and she'd go through fuel quickly. Every month she'd had to forage a little further out to find kindling. Last year she'd been forced to purchase bundles of wood in town during the coldest months.

"God," she spoke into the blue sky, "I've been ungrateful, and I have no right to ask for anything, but I really need help right now. Orrie needs a warm coat, shoes--and so many other things. What do I do?"

Suddenly, she felt silly. With all the things going on in the world, presidents and kings and wars and who knew what else, why would God want to help her?

Gruff, a medium-sized yellow mutt who'd wandered up to the house a few months ago and refused to leave, gave his 'here comes a friend' bark.

"Shh, you silly dog. Orrie's sleeping late this morning!"

The dog bounded up to her, his tongue hanging out of his mouth. She patted him on his scruffy head. Yes, another mouth to feed, but he paid for his keep by alerting her to every human and beastly visitor.

Gravel scattered under hooves on the path.

"Good job, Gruff," she whispered.

A dazzling piebald pony galloped around the corner. The animal slowed as it reached the yard. Soonie swung down. Today she wore buckskins and her hair flowed over her shoulders.

"Wylder told me about the corn man." She walked over to Zillia's wood stack and nudged it with her toe. "You're gonna get cold. There's not enough wood around here to keep you going. By

January it'll be gone."

Zillia frowned. "I know, but what can I do? I don't even have money for flour this year. Maybe I can barter for a few loads of wood."

"I came by to tell you. Mrs. Slolem is making pecan pies, and she wanted more nuts. She'll pay a good price if they are shelled and ready."

"Pecans? But we only have two trees." Zillia pointed to the small specimens that grew in the lawn. "I won't have enough to sell."

"Yes, but I found a grove."

"An entire grove? Is it on someone's property?" Zillia clasped her hands in front of her.

Soonie nodded. "Old Mr. Dunbar. I met him in the store yesterday. He asked if I'd like to help him harvest his grove in return for half of the nuts. He's getting on in years and can't afford a crew. I think we could gather several bushels."

Zillia's fingers ached when she thought of the countless hours they'd spend plucking meat from the sharp shells. Shelled pecans fetched a much better price than whole ones. "I'm finished with the animals. The rest of the chores can wait. I'll go wake Orrie."

Soonie skipped beside her like a little girl as she walked towards the house. "Wylder and Grandpa are harvesting the early pumpkins today, but we can take the small wagon."

Zillia gathered the few empty barrels and baskets scattered around the house and stacked them by the door.

When she went into Mama's room, which she now shared with Orrie, her brother was sitting up in his little cot. Blue eyes widened, and he stared at her like she was part of a dream.

"Want to go into the woods with Aunt Soonie?" she asked.

Orrie nodded in solemn silence. When he climbed out of bed his diaper sagged.

Zillia poked her head into the kitchen. "Soonie, it'll be a minute. Someone had too much water before bed last night."

Soonie frowned. "He still wets the bed? My cousins were going to the privy before they were his age."

Good for them. Soonie was her best friend, but it irritated her to no end when people compared Orrie to other children.

Zillia jerked the covers off the cot. The sickly-sweet odor made her nose wrinkle. She poured water into the basin, cleaned Orrie up and dressed him quickly. "Every child is different," Grandma Louise always said when Zillia came to her with concerns.

The wet clothing and sheets went into a basket. Tomorrow was laundry day. Orrie could sleep in her bed tonight. She'd have to limit drinks so he didn't soak them both.

"All right, we're ready," she said to Soonie, who was flipping through a battered book of fairy tales she had pulled off the shelf.

"Good. Let's go."

Soonie lifted Orrie up on the pony's back and held the bridle while she led them on the fifteen-minute walk back to her house. The cool of the morning was still upon them. The sun was watered down by colors and not to its full brightness.

Once in the Eckhart's barn, the girls worked quickly to hitch the mare to the small wagon and load up their baskets and barrels. On the way out, they met Wylder coming in on the buckboard full of round, ripe pumpkins.

His eyes softened when he saw Zillia. He nodded towards the fruit. "These will fetch a good price in town. Hard to believe it's already time to make pumpkin pie."

"Autumn did come quickly this year." Zillia jumped out of the small wagon and leaned over the side of the buckboard to examine the crop. "You'll save me a pumpkin, right?"

"Only if you make me a pie."

Zillia's smile froze. A pie? She'd never attempted such a thing. Grandma Louise had already spent hours teaching her to make Johnny cake, bread and preserves. Before Mama died, the only thing she had cooked was toasted bread on a fork. "Um... Of course I will."

Soonie raised her eyebrows, but she didn't say anything.

Wylder pulled the reins a little tighter. "Soonie, are you sure y'all should be going out in the woods alone today? Mr. Bell sighted a panther a few miles upriver and those creatures can swim. If you wait, perhaps I can go with you tomorrow."

Zillia's mouth fell open. "Wylder, we go out by ourselves all the time!"

Soonie pulled a shotgun from the seat behind her. "Who's the best shot? Want to try to beat me right now? You haven't been able to do it yet."

Wylder ducked his head and smiled. "That's true. Zillia's not too bad either. Just be careful, please." He clicked to his team and the wagon jolted into the barn.

Zillia climbed up beside Soonie and rolled her eyes. "I can take care of myself."

"He wants to make sure we stay safe." Soonie slapped the reins across the mare's back and the horse plodded down the road.

"I know." Zillia sat back. "I just don't like it. What makes men think they are superior anyway? We are all made of the same flesh and bone."

"True," Soonie said. "But Wylder doesn't think he's better than anyone else. He worries about you, that's all."

"He doesn't have to worry!" Zillia knew Soonie was right, but she couldn't hold back her words. "We've been fine!"

"He did have to fish you out of the river." Soonie's tone remained even. "You can't always do everything for yourself, no matter how strong you are."

"Oooh!" Zillia bit the inside of her cheek and stumbled from the front of the wagon to join Orrie in the back. She sat down hard beside him.

Tall and beautiful in the buckboard seat, Soonie looked like she could take on anything on her own. She shook her head slightly but did not glance back.

Zillia sighed and folded her arms. Disturbing thoughts crept into her mind, and not for the first time. *Why do Soonie and*

Wylder bother? I'm just an added burden, not even family.

Soonie chanted to herself in Comanche while Orrie played with stones. Neither seemed to notice her brooding. Zillia knew better than to allow herself to wade too deep into the mire of self-pity. Once there, it would be hard to get out.

She reached out and touched Soonie's shoulder. "I'm sorry I was mad. You were right. I am so grateful for everything you and your family have done for me. I just wish I knew how to pay you back."

"It's been a hard time for you," Soonie said. "But you are brave, and God will see you through. Our treasures await in Heaven."

"I'm sure there's a whole palace waiting for you."

Soonie turned to her. "I just want to see His face." Her eyes shimmered, like they did every time she talked about her faith. "That will be enough for me."

When they reached the pecan bottoms, Zillia's bad mood disappeared.

Trees created tunnels before them, with glimmers of fall sunshine leaking through. Birds called out warnings and squirrels scampered across the path. Patches of flowers brightened spots in yellow defiance to the approaching winter. And the ground was littered with thousands of pecans.

Soonie jumped down and picked up a handful of the small, oval shaped pecans. Cracking two together, she picked out the meat. "Here," She handed half to Zillia. "See what you think."

Zillia bit into the wrinkled meat. "Delicious! I've never had a better one."

"Mrs. Slolem will be pleased." Soonie beamed. "Let's get to work."

The two girls worked in haste to fill their containers. A few times Orrie threw in a fistful of twigs and leaves, but most of the time he was content to play with his rocks.

By noon, the girls had filled every container and stood by the wagon, ready to drive to the house of Mr. Dunbar and deliver his share.

Zillia handed Orrie a chunk of Johnny cake. He stuffed a big piece into his mouth and his cheeks bulged out.

Soonie pointed to the brown creatures gathering nuts across the forest floor. "You look like a squirrel, Orrie."

"You do." Zillia laughed. "Don't eat so much at once, dear, or you'll choke."

Orrie laughed too, and crumbs poured out of his mouth.

Soonie stood and began to twirl beneath the trees. Her fringed skirt swirled around her ankles while she danced to a melody she hummed under her breath.

"Are you singing a Comanche song?" Zillia asked.

"No." Soonie's hair flew out while she jumped and spun. She pulled a scarf away from where it was looped around her neck and began to swing it in graceful arcs over her head. "It's a song I made up. For God."

Zillia frowned. "I thought God only wanted us to sing in

church. Like hymns."

Soonie continued to dance. Her song was wild and full of joy, nothing like the somber hymns they sang every Sunday among the stiff wooden pews.

After a few moments, Soonie stopped and came to plop down between Orrie and Zillia. Her cheeks glowed and her eyes shone. "Wylder and I read about King David and how he danced before God. Psalms commands us to sing new songs to the Lord. When we were younger, we would come out to the woods to dance and sing for God. It always made us feel closer to Him."

Zillia gave Soonie an apple from the lunch basket. "I can't picture Wylder dancing like that."

Soonie lowered her eyes. "Well, he doesn't do it anymore. At least, not around other folks. But he still makes up songs. Much better than mine."

"I've heard him." Zillia found an apple for herself. "Sometimes, when he doesn't know I'm listening. I thought those were old songs from your grandparent's country."

"No." Soonie picked Orrie up and set him down in the wagon. "Let's head home. If we get chores done soon enough, we might have time to shell some of these before supper."

On the way home, Orrie fell asleep on Zillia's shoulder, his blond curls tangling with her brown braids, which had come unpinned during the work day.

Maybe God doesn't mind if we make up our own songs. She frowned. *Maybe He wants us to sing songs that we have written for*

Him. A person wrote the hymns, someone wrote the Psalms. What made those people more special to God than anyone else? Perhaps she could ask Pastor Fowler. He did seem open to new ideas.

She pictured the pastor deep in thought, with his bushy black eyebrows drawn together over his hawk-like nose. *Maybe I'll just look it up for myself.*

Most of the time, she didn't touch the dusty family Bible except to take it to church on Sundays. But she hated when Soonie knew about things she didn't. *Does the Bible really talk about dancing?*

After the pecans, she would read Psalms for herself.

NOVEMBER 1888

7

Baking Day

The melody tripped along with the squeak of the rocker while the late fall winds howled outside.

> *"Down in the Valley*
> *valley so low,*
> *hang your head over,*
> *hear the wind blow.*
> *Hear the wind blow, boy,*
> *hear the wind blow,*
> *hang your head over,*

hear the wind blow

Zillia shivered, whether at the thought of another winter coming or from her own haunting song, she wasn't sure. When these cold spells hit, Zillia and Orrie stayed by the kitchen fire all night to save fuel. They cuddled together in the rocker, though Orrie was far too big to be rocked and sometimes her legs fell asleep before he did.

The pecans had brought in enough money to pay for food for them and grain for the animals, but she still didn't know what to do about winter clothes. Soonie's nephews wore their clothes out as fast as Grandma Louise could sew them. This seemed to be the case with every boy in River County, so she didn't have much luck with hand-me-downs.

The house didn't feel as cold as last night. Zillia struggled to pull herself to her feet with Orrie, limp with sleep, in her arms.

Gruff stretched and got up to follow them. His toenails clicked on the floor behind her. He sniffed beneath the table, checking for any stray crumbs from dinner.

Zillia staggered to Orrie's little cot and pulled the blanket back with her foot. Earlier she had wrapped a hot brick in a cloth and placed it under the covers. She nudged it to the foot of the bed with her toes.

After tucking Orrie into bed, she went through the kitchen and into the small pantry. Gruff followed her in with bedraggled ears perked, his tail waving like a corn tassel.

Zillia surveyed rows of gleaming jars. Some she traded for, but most were vegetables and fruits from her own garden. "Don't give me those sad eyes!" she said to the dog. "You already had your dinner!"

Two jars glowed bright orange in the lantern light, despite being shoved on the farthest top shelf.

Wylder hadn't mentioned the pumpkin pie again, even when he'd rolled the brightest, bounciest specimen onto her porch. Still, she had promised. *After everything he's done for us.* Days of unpaid labor, haunches of meat he could have traded or sold. He'd saved her life, for goodness sake. All this time, he had only asked for one thing.

Her pie-making attempts had resulted in burned squiggles of crusts. Even the chickens had ignored the pitiful bits she flung into the yard.

Thanksgiving was in two days. She sank down into the rocker and rubbed her temples. Every holiday, she and Orrie would go to the Eckharts' cabin. And there would be pie, all different kinds. Her fingers dug into the arms of the chair and she set her jaw. She would make a brilliant pie, even if the house burnt down in the process. There wouldn't be a single singed crumb for anyone to laugh about. In the words of Grandpa Walt, she was 'sick unto tarnation' of people's lopsided smiles of pity.

This time, mouths would hang open in awe and wonder.

"Just you wait, Wylder Eckhart," she whispered into the empty cabin. "I'll make you the most beautiful pie in River

County!"

The next morning. she woke, stiff and cold in the rocking chair. Daylight streamed through worn muslin curtains. *How do I keep falling asleep in here?* Her back ached.

Pie day.

When she went to check on Orrie, he still snored beneath Mama's homemade quilt. Tiptoeing to the bed, she ran a finger over the rough, uneven stitches. Though the quilt had its flaws, Mama had been so proud of it. "The first one I ever made," she had told Zillia. "It took me an entire year. I finished while I was waiting for you to come. You kept kicking the patches off my lap."

The pie doesn't have to be perfect, she decided when she reached the kitchen. She spooned lard into a bowl. *It just has to be a pie.*

Salt, just a pinch, then she added in flour a handful at a time, like Grandma Louise had shown her. A little more lard, then she pushed and pinched until dough formed in a blob between her fingers. Already, this crust had a smoother consistency than any of her previous attempts. She sprinkled flour on the table and rolled out the dough. The lump cracked and separated, but when she placed the pieces in the pie tin she dabbed a little water on the edges. Miraculously, it helped smooth them together.

The golden chunks of pumpkin shone while she poured them into a separate dish. She added eggs, sugar and milk. Pie mixture ran into the crust and settled in a thick, amber pool. The rich spicy scent filled the air. She placed into the stove and carefully closed the door. Maybe, just maybe, this time the dessert would turn out all right.

"Zilly, I'm waked up." Orrie bawled from the door, his pearly teeth flashing.

"All right. Well, let's find some breakfast then, shall we?" She broke off a piece of the eternal johnny-cake and held it out to him.

He folded his arms and glared. "No cake."

"How about some grits? With molasses?"

"No grits."

"I'll look in the pantry, but I don't think we have anything else, honey."

Orrie sniffed the air. "What smells?"

"I'm making pie, for Thanksgiving."

His lips curved up at the corners. "I want pie."

"No, Orrie," she sighed. "We're taking the pie to the Eckhart's house tomorrow. Don't you remember? We're supposed to share."

"I want pie!"

She grabbed a plate, plunked the piece of johnny cake on it, and drizzled molasses over the food. The dish clattered on the table when she set it down. "Eat it or starve," she growled.

Orrie's blue eyes brimmed with tears. "Mean Zilly."

Someone pounded on the door. Zilly hurried over to answer it. As she slid back the bolt, a piece of johnny cake thudded against the wall. She rolled her eyes and swung the door open.

Wylder leaned against the frame, his broad-brimmed hat in hand. "Zillia, sorry to bother you, but I noticed the goats were out.

I'll probably need help herding them back in." He studied her over the muffler she had knit for him last Christmas. One end was wider than the other and a few strange knobs stuck out where the yarn had snarled.

I'm staring again. She tucked a curl behind her ear. "How did they get out this time? We fixed that fence days ago."

"Don't know. Grandpa and I heard howls by the cabin last night. That's why I came by." He sniffed the air like Orrie had and gave her his lopsided grin. "Something sure smells good."

"I've heard howling too, for a week now."

Wylder frowned. "Why didn't you tell us? I would have come to look."

I've been out watching for them. Zillia didn't want a lecture on the dangers of patrolling the farm at night. She threw on Papa's coat and hat and fetched her brother's sweater. "Come on, Orrie, we have to go find the goats again."

"I want pie." Orrie folded his arms and stuck out his lower lip. Despite his protests, Zillia pulled the sweater over his head and jammed his arms into the sleeves.

Wylder's lips twitched and his eyes twinkled.

Zillia smiled apologetically. "Sorry, we've had a rough morning."

"Aw, I'm used to it. We have two little boys at home, remember? Though Grandpa Walt might've tanned a hide by now." He squinted at Orrie.

Orrie glared right back.

Out in the yard, a few curled leaves still clung to the oak trees with hopeful twigs. Pinecones dotted the thick carpet of brown needles under the stand of pines. Hundreds of black birds, only seen when the chill air started, swooped and landed on any available perch.

When the three of them reached the goat pen, only a few of the oldest nannies huddled in the stall. A scattering of cloven prints told the story; the other dozen goats had found a weak board in the fence and pressed against the wood until it broke free.

"We're lucky they prefer to stick together. If we find one, we'll find them all." Wylder bent down in front of Zillia to examine the fence more closely. Today he smelled like the smoke house. Bacon, ham, and turkey, plus his normal Wylder self.

Why should I care what he smells like? I'm going crazy. Zillia's fingers crept up to her blazing cheeks. Good thing he couldn't read her thoughts. She shook her head and examined the tracks, Orrie in tow. "They get out all the time. Hopefully they'll find an area with lots of grapevine." The goats couldn't resist the tender vines.

"Doesn't look like they've been out long." Wylder glanced up. "I'm going to repair this fence so the others don't escape. It'll just take a minute." He grabbed a rock and began pounding the nails back into the board.

"Wylder, I'm worried about that howling we heard. I'm going on ahead to find them." Zillia slung her gun over her shoulder and turned toward the path.

"Wait for me. You don't want to deal with varmints on your own."

Truly? She folded her arms in front of her chest and gave Wylder a cold stare, which he didn't notice. "I'm going now, you take all the time you need if you think this fence is so important."

Wylder pounded harder.

"Fine. Orrie, let's go."

Orrie squinted up at her. "I'm cold."

Wylder banged the last nail in. He swung Orrie up on his shoulders. "Come on, let's look for some goats." He strode past Zillia without giving her a glance. The little boy squealed in delight while they marched through the woods.

Only a few moments passed before they heard crashes in the brush. "Just like I thought," Zillia sighed. "Back to their favorite patch."

"Wait." Wylder put his hand out in front of her. "Pretty sure I heard a dog."

"See? I knew we should have come faster," Zillia said. A pack of dogs could take down a flock in minutes, and unlike coyotes, they weren't afraid of people.

Wylder lowered Orrie to the ground and pulled his Colt pistol out of its holster. Zillia followed him into the clearing.

Two nannies with black and white spots ran towards them, bleating in terror.

Three large hounds had the buck up against a tree. The frightened goat lowered his head in attempt to fend them off with his horns, but blood streamed from gashes on his muzzle.

A fourth dog turned toward them. A kid goat's lifeless body dangled from his jaws.

Angry tears stung Zillia's eyes. The baby goat, Sammy, had been Orrie's favorite. She pushed the little boy behind her and steadied her gun.

The shot ripped through the air. The fourth dog jerked back and dropped its victim. It rolled over and lay still.

Dogs and goats scattered into the forest.

Orrie struggled to get away. "Dogs hurt Sammy!"

"Stay with me, Orrie. Those dogs could bite you, too." Zillia's heart pounded in her chest. What if the beasts had come into the farmyard while Orrie was playing outside?

Wylder walked over to the dog she had shot and nudged it with his boot. "We don't have to worry about this one any more. I'm going to go after the other three; you try to get as many goats in as possible."

"Be careful." Zillia pulled Orrie close against her. The little boy shivered and buried his face in her coat. "Come on, dear. We have to be brave now. Let's try to find the other goats."

One nanny had already returned to nose the body of the kid. Zillia grabbed her horns and led her back down the path. Two nannies trotted in behind them. The buck and two babies waited for them when their unusual parade reached the fence. *Only two more missing. Hopefully they'll come back as well.* After Zillia shooed them into the stall, she slammed the door. They'd have to stay inside until she found a way to make the fence stronger.

Horse hooves clattered and spurs jingled in the south field. Three Trent brothers, with Abel in the lead.

Zillia's muscles tightened. *What are they doing here?*

Abel hefted his huge body off his horse. "Couple of my dogs got loose and we need 'em for a hunt. Have you seen 'em?"

Zillia's fists clenched at her sides. "Should've known those mangy mutts were yours, Abel Trent! They came after my goats and killed one of the babies. I shot one, and I hope Wylder got the rest."

"Which one did you shoot?" Abel stepped towards her.

Zillia stood her ground. "The one that decided to kill Orrie's favorite goat."

Abel's brother, Ed, dismounted and came up to her. "Missy, those dogs are premium coon hunters." He squinted. eyes absurdly tiny in the flabby folds of his face. "Worth far more than your raggedy goats."

"Goat killers are worth nothing, and the sheriff will agree with me."

A reddish hue crept up from Ed's collar and over his face. He opened his mouth to reply, right as Wylder strolled through the trees.

"Is there a problem?" Wylder asked.

"Did you track them down?" Zillia hadn't heard any shots, but she still hoped.

"Unfortunately, no." He looked over at Abel. "Figured those

were yours. They high-tailed it to Edgar Billing's land. You'd better get over there before they bother his prize-winning dairy cows."

"How do I know you're telling the truth, half-breed?"

Wylder's knuckles turned white as his fingers tightened around the stick he still carried. "Your dogs aren't here, Abel. Leave us alone. If we see them again, they'll be dealt with accordingly."

Abel looked at the stick and then at Wylder's face.

Zillia closed her eyes. Wylder had trounced Abel more than once, but Abel was with his brothers. *Please, please leave.*

Dogs howled and barked once more, farther to the north this time. Abel nodded to the other men. They all mounted their horses and rode off without another word.

Wylder stood straight and still, watching until they disappeared into the trees.

Zillia's hands shook. *I can't let evil people intimidate me. I'm not a little girl anymore. If I'm going to survive, I must fight for what I want.* She gulped a few breaths of the crisp, fall air and reached down for Orrie. "Come on, let's get you warm."

A cloud of smoke hit her face when she opened the door. "Oh no, not the pie!" She fanned the smoke out of her face and rushed to pull open the oven. Pan and pastry had become a blackened mess.

Out went the smoking thing to the porch steps, right as Wylder came up to the door.

"Keep your ears open for those dogs. I'll report them to the sheriff, but after a taste of freedom they are going to be hard to catch. You always take your gun with you outside, right?"

She nodded.

He lifted his chin towards the burnt pastry. "What's that?"

"Your pie." Zillia lowered her head.

"Aw, Zillia, you really made me a pie?"

"I wanted to." Her fingers curled in her coat pockets. "I tried."

He knelt to examine the charred object. "Well, the crust crinkled up real good."

"Why are you so nice to me?" she burst out. "You ask for one thing, and I can't even do it right! After all you and your family have done for us, I could never, ever pay you back." Her lips trembled, and she struggled to hold herself together.

Wylder stood and stared at her for a moment. Then he placed a gloved hand on her shoulder. "It's been a tough day, Zillia. You're such a little spitfire, you know that?" His eyes shone as he studied her face. "You're my friend. I will always be here when you need me."

For some reason, this only made her feel worse. She turned away so he wouldn't see her frustration. "Thank you," she managed. "Do you think... you could bury Sammy? I don't want Orrie to have to see."

"Of course. I'm happy to help you."

Her heart melted into a puddle of guilt as her shaky fingers brushed the end of his knobby muffler. She turned back through the door.

He followed her and stood on the threshold. "Well," he said finally. "I'll see you tomorrow. Please don't fret about the pie. You tried your best."

The door closed behind him. She sank into a chair and pulled her hat down over her face. "What a horrible, horrible day."

Orrie tugged on her sleeve. His eyes were round and hopeful in his dirty, tear-streaked face. "Zilly, can I have pie?"

8

The Hat Shop

Soonie pointed at the "Help Wanted" sign as they passed the door of the hat shop after church. "The store must be doing well if Mrs. Purpose is hiring."

"I suppose so," Zillia said. She had never been inside. The merchandise was far too expensive. Mama had always trimmed their hats, even when they could have afforded to pay someone else.

She reached out to trace the fancy curled letters. "Soonie, maybe I could work here."

"Perhaps." Soonie shrugged. "But how would you manage everything else? You already have so much to do."

"It's almost Christmas, we don't have any crops. I could get up earlier to feed and milk the goats. Pay someone to care for Orrie." Zillia clasped her hands together. "Oh, Soonie, this could help so much!"

"Maybe."

Zillia tugged Orrie over to Grandma Louise, who was talking with a friend. "Grandma, could you watch him for a moment? I need to run back into church."

"Of course. Don't be long now; beans are on the stove."

Zillia hurried past the shops, all decorated with bows and stars for Christmas, to the church porch.

Mrs. Purpose was reaching out a chubby, white hand covered with jewels to shake Pastor Fowler's thin, tan one. "Lovely sermon, as always," she said.

Pastor Fowler beamed.

Why doesn't he smile during his teachings? Zillia remembered Soonie, dancing for the Lord under the trees. What would Pastor Fowler have to say about that? Maybe he wouldn't approve. But it was right there in the Bible, Zillia had read the verses for herself.

"Did you have a question, Miss. Bright?" Pastor Fowler asked kindly.

"Oh," Zillia stammered. "I need to speak to Mrs. Purpose. When she has a moment."

Mrs. Purpose's powder white eyebrows traveled up the brim of her hat, which was adorned with false cherries, a strange bird, and what must be ostrich plumes. "Yes, Zillia, what can I do for you?"

"I saw the sign in your shop's window. You're looking for help?"

Mrs. Purpose looked her over, eyes lingering on Zillia's shabby clothes, worn shoes, and gloveless fingers. "Well, yes. I do need some help around the store. A hat trimmer, to be precise. Do you know someone with experience?"

"Yes, ma'am. I would like the job."

"Don't you run a farm?" Mrs. Purpose wrinkled her nose.

"Now, Mrs. Purpose, I'm sure she would do quite well." Pastor Fowler nodded at Zillia.

"She certainly would," said a gentle voice. Mrs. Fowler, the pastor's wife, had come up behind her. The tall, willowy woman laid a gloved hand on Zillia's shoulder. "Why, this girl plowed two acres of river land in a day. Isn't that right?"

"Yes Ma'am, I do my best." Zillia's words flowed faster in her excitement. "My mama taught me how to sew and I learn quickly. I helped her trim hats for years, especially when we lived in Alexandria."

Mrs. Purpose squinted. "That's right. I remember some of the hats your ma wore. A bit simple, but lovely work. Well, I suppose I could give you a try. I've had a hard time finding someone for the job. Most of the men in town don't want their womenfolk working in a shop, even though it's perfectly respectable."

"There's no one to object in my case." Zillia smiled.

"It's probably for the best, Dearie." Mrs. Purpose gave a curt nod. "Men can be bothersome."

Mrs. Fowler covered her smile with a lace handkerchief.

Pastor Fowler frowned.

"Be at my shop by eight am tomorrow. Sharp." Mrs. Purpose glared at her over wire-rimmed spectacles. "I don't abide tardiness."

"Yes, Ma'am." Zillia ducked her head and almost tripped in her haste down the porch steps. She caught herself and slowed to a walk. She didn't want Mrs. Purpose to think she was too wild and impulsive to work in her store.

After she plopped into the wagon next to Orrie, she told everyone her news.

Grandma Louise tilted her head back and frowned. "I know you need money, but do you think working in town is the best way?"

"Well, at least I'll have four new walls to stare at all day. And something different to occupy my time." *Why can't they see how this can help me?*

Soonie touched her arm. "Zillia, have you thought about selling the farm? You've kept this up for over two years now. Maybe it would be best to let it go."

"Don't you think I've considered that?" Zillia didn't mean the words to come out so sharp, but once begun, they were hard to stop. "Jeb would definitely try to stop me, if word reached whatever jail he's locked up in. Even if I could manage to sell the land where would I go? My relatives in the East don't want me. There's no one but the Trents, and I'd rather die than live under the same roof as Jemima, wouldn't you?" A tear slid down her cheek and she scrubbed it away with a worn handkerchief. *I can't let go of Papa's farm. It's the last thing I have to hold onto.*

Soonie bit her lip and stared down at the reins. "I know, Zillia. But Wylder will be gone this spring and I'm not sure what I'll be doing now school's finished. We won't be able to help you anymore."

"Wylder is going away?" Zillia choked out.

"Yes." Grandma Louise's eyes crinkled at the corners, and Zillia couldn't tell if her smile was happy or just brave. "He's taking a job with a new lumber camp upriver. He didn't tell you?"

Zillia's fingers tightened around the wagon seat. "No, he didn't." Well, it wasn't like he had to tell her every detail of his life. It wasn't really her business. *Right?*

All her excitement about the new job floated away in the breeze like dandelion seeds. She laid her head on her arms and left her neck to the wagon's jolting mercy.

"Zilly, are you okay?" Orrie peeked under her arm.

"Yes, sweetheart. I'm just tired."

The next morning, two hours earlier than usual, Zillia milked the goats, fed the chickens, and packed bread and a jar of pickles in her Sunday basket. Then she and Orrie began the hour walk to town.

Soonie always referred to this sort of morning as "a golden day," unseasonably warm, with brilliant rays of sun filtering through branches bereft of finery.

Zillia was thankful for the fine weather, but she couldn't help but wonder how they would make the journey on colder mornings. She would have to cut up an old blanket or two and improvise jackets for both her and Orrie. *I certainly can't wear Papa's coat to town.*

Thirty minutes later, Zillia knocked on the door of Mrs. Kent's home. The woman had three children of her own. She had agreed to care for Orrie in exchange for eggs and butter.

A fit of coughing met her ears through the thick wood. The handle turned and the door cracked just enough to reveal Mrs. Kent's white face. The lady wiped sweat off her forehead with a dirty apron. "We all have colds today, Zillia, and little Davey has the fever." She looked down at Orrie and gave a weak smile. "I don't want him to be catchin' our ailment."

Zillia's heart thudded to the dust. What would she do with her brother? "All right, Mrs. Kent. Hope you all feel better."

She took Orrie's hand and led him back to the road. "You'll have to behave yourself and come with me today, just this once."

He gave her an angelic smile.

Despite the early hour, the town of Bastrop bustled with activity. Customers stood in line outside the butcher shop and bakery, waiting for the first pick of fresh meat and bread. Wagons trundled down the road toward the end of town, where farmers gathered to market their goods once a week.

River was a good-sized town, boasting cotton gins, a bank, several stores, four churches and two schools. Papa had chosen River because he knew Mama wanted to remain close to 'civilization' as she had called it. Zillia remembered how fun trips to town used to be, when they could walk into any shop and purchase anything they wanted. *I didn't even realize how spoiled I was.*

When Mrs. Purpose opened the door of her store, she stared down at Orrie as if he were a rabbit coming to eat her prized cabbages. Her lips drew into a thin line. "My shop is for ladies. Children do not belong here."

Zillia's first attempt at speech failed. She swallowed hard and tried again. "I really need this job. Please give me a chance."

Mrs. Purpose's eyes softened. She tapped her fingers against her double chin. "I must stay up front to assist customers. You will have work in the back, still watching him every moment."

Too thankful to speak, Zillia simply nodded.

"Come on in." Mrs. Purpose swept through the front door. A little bell tinkled over Zillia and Orrie's heads when they followed her into the store.

"Don't touch anything," Zillia hissed down at Orrie, whose eyes had doubled in size.

He bobbed his head, a finger stuck in his mouth. When she had to go into a shop, she would normally leave him outside with someone. She wasn't quite sure how he would react to this strange new environment.

They threaded though tables topped with lacy bonnets, straw hats with ribbons to tie under one's chin, stovepipe hats for gentlemen, and the latest rage... bowlers, brought down from New York. She was glad she came bareheaded. Mrs. Purpose would have had a fit of vapors if she saw her in Papa's old broad-brimmed hat.

A wooden counter rose at the back of the shop, topped by measuring devices and sample hats for custom fittings. A mirror in a golden frame hung on the wall.

A quick look in the glass and Zillia turned away. During the long walk a thin layer of dust had powdered her face and her collar was stained with sweat. No wonder Mrs. Purpose wanted her to work in the back. She patted her curls in attempt to put them back into some form of order.

Mrs. Purpose pulled back a fabric curtain to reveal a small door behind the counter. She beckoned to Zillia. "Come, you'll be working in here."

The room was larger than the store front, and much less tidy. Tables and shelves overflowed with laces, ribbons and fabrics.

"You can see my last employee wasn't much for order," Mrs. Purpose sniffed. "But she was a genius in the art of hattery. Alas, she married an insufferable man and went away to San Antonio."

A box of hats clattered to the floor, and Mrs. Purpose stacked them back again. "Your first task will be to clean and organize this area. I don't care how you arrange everything; just make sure it's manageable. I would have taken the task myself, but I've been far too busy with customers to trouble myself with this chaos."

The bell tinkled and she bustled back towards the door. "See what you can do while I'm gone." She closed it in her wake.

Zillia surveyed the space. Order had been absent from this area for quite some time, it would take several hours to make it right again.

"Might as well get started, Orrie." A few, small, empty spools where piled on the counter. She handed these to him. "Look, you can put these on this ribbon, like this."

"O.k."

Much larger spools were lined against the wall, most holding ribbon and lace. The contents of these were partially unwound and tangled together on the floor. She chose a spool of lovely green satin thread to start with. Patiently, she followed the ribbon, unsnarling it from the mess inch by inch. A sense of satisfaction filled her as each loop of ribbon smoothed back into place. Settling into a rhythm, she finished the green silk and began on a filmy lace, so fragile she feared it would dissolve in her fingers. A smile played on her lips. It had been a long time since she'd had the chance to touch such beautiful things. Now here she was, surrounded by finery.

Wouldn't it be wonderful if she could keep this job? What if Mrs. Purpose offered her a raise, right away? What if she made her a partner? They could afford new coats, maybe even some things for the house. *We could get the pump fixed. And repair the cracked walls.*

Five spools finished. The pile was almost gone. What should she work on next? She brushed a square of crimson velvet against her cheek.

A woman's shriek interrupted her reverie. She glanced up. Spools lay scattered on the floor. No Orrie.

"Oh no," she whispered. Pushing the pile of ribbons from her lap, she jumped up and hurried through the door.

At first, all she saw were feathers. Soft, fluffy, and sticking to every surface in the room. Four feather-covered shapes jumped and shrieked around the counter. Arms waved wildly to clear the air of quills.

One person was much smaller than the others.

"Zilly!" Orrie ran toward her, his mouth drawn with fear. "Big chickens!"

The larger three, Zillia realized in horror, were Mrs. Purpose, Mrs. Trent, and Mrs. Fowler. They stopped hopping about and stared at her.

"I'm so sorry." Zillia bent down to scoop up a handful of feathers. Most of them escaped her grasp and settled on various perches in the room. "I don't know how he got away from me so fast. I promise I'll clean everything up."

Mrs. Fowler knelt down to smile at Orrie. "Haven't I seen you at church?"

Orrie beamed. "Yep."

Mrs. Trent brushed feathers off her dress as though they were cockroaches. "You brought him to work with you? How could you be so irresponsible?" She turned to Mrs. Purpose. "What did I tell you? Absolutely not a fit guardian for a child." She glared at Zillia.

"Yes, I see. Please forgive the state of our store today, Mrs. Trent. I promise you will never be subjected to this sort of treatment again." Mrs. Purpose ushered the still feather-covered Jemima Trent out the door.

On the way back, Mrs. Purpose pulled a handful of quills from the brim of a bowler where they had settled. "Five dollars' worth of fine feathers. Spoiled."

Mrs. Fowler laughed. "Surely a bit of floating didn't hurt them. Here, we'll all work together. We can clean this up in a few moments." She bent down in her smart, gray suit and began to scoop feathers back into the bag.

Orrie helped Zillia pull feathers from displays.

Mrs. Purpose scraped feathers off her clothes, fussing to herself.

"Whatever possessed you to throw all these feathers around?" Zillia asked her brother. Even with their best efforts, a few stragglers still floated in lazy patterns around the room.

"I wanted a chicken." Orrie peered into the bag.

"I think that's the best we can do." Mrs. Fowler handed the sack to Mrs. Purpose. "Most of these are none the worse for the wear." She pulled a dollar out of her purse and placed it on the counter. "This should cover any spoiled ones, shouldn't it?"

"I suppose." Mrs. Purpose took the bill and placed it in her cash box. She crossed her arms and turned to Zillia. "I hope you understand, you will have to find employment somewhere else."

A lump rose in Zillia's throat, but she couldn't think of a single argument, so she just nodded. "Thanks for letting me try."

"Good day." Mrs. Purpose held the door open and Zillia and Orrie followed Mrs. Fowler out into the street.

The temperature had fallen and the sun was hidden behind an ominous black cloud.

Mrs. Fowler shivered. "I think winter decided to blow through. I'd say it's a cider day." She smiled at Orrie. "How about it? would you like some hot apple cider?"

"Don't know." Orrie scrunched up his face.

"He's never tried it, ma'am," said Zillia.

"We'll fix that." Mrs. Fowler shook out her heavy woolen skirts, and a few more feathers flew out on the street. "Come with me." She marched in the direction of the general store.

"Ma'am." The words stuck in Zillia's throat. "I'll have to ask you to wait a few weeks, but I'll pay you back for those feathers. And I can't afford cider right now." Her stomach twisted. *Where am I going to get the money?* She wanted to crawl into a rain barrel and never come out.

"Pooh! What's a tiny thing like that among friends? Besides, I couldn't sleep tonight if I knew this child had gone another day without trying apple cider. It simply isn't decent! And don't fret too much about what happened," Mrs. Fowler said over her shoulder. "My little brother used to get me into all sorts of trouble, once upon a time."

Zillia sighed while she followed Mrs. Fowler into the store. Though she appreciated her kindness, she doubted very much the woman held the same relationship and responsibility for her brother that she had with Orrie.

Lanterns hung from hooks in the dry goods store to illuminate shelves of merchandise. Bunches of dried herbs dangled from the rafters and filled the air with tangy scents that tickled Zillia's nose.

Mrs. Fowler stepped up to the counter. Despite her forty-plus years, her eyes sparkled like a young girl. "Three hot apple ciders, please, Mr. Bolter." She placed two shiny coins on the counter.

The shopkeeper nodded, his spectacles rattling. "I have a fresh batch just now, Mrs. Fowler." He pulled three mugs from under the counter and ladled out steaming liquid from a cast iron kettle on the stove. He handed the mugs to each of them. "Don't drink too fast; you'll burn your tongues."

Steam hit Orrie's face when he peered inside his mug. "Ow!"

"Careful, Orrie. Blow on it, like hot grits."

When Zillia's drink had cooled, she tried to take small sips to make the spicy sweetness last. Sugar and fruit had been dear this year, so she savored the unexpected treat.

Mrs. Fowler's kind brown eyes studied Zillia over the rim of her cup. She drained the last bit and set it down on the counter. "You haven't had much time for fun lately, have you, dear?"

Unexpected tears smarted in Zillia's eyes. She blinked them away and looked down. "I suppose not, Ma'am. I don't really think about it much."

"Of course not." Mrs. Fowler patted Zillia's hand. "You don't have time, do you? What about school? Were you able to complete your studies?"

"Mama planned to send me to a finishing school back east. Before Papa died. That's when everything changed."

"Don't feel too bad." A tiny smile played around the corner of Mrs. Fowler's mouth. "My experience with finishing school, though quite long ago, was terrible. A blasted place full of snobby, silly girls and headmistresses with switches."

Should a pastor's wife say such things? Zillia had to rest her chin on her hand to keep her jaw from dropping. "I never really wanted to go away, but Mama thought it would be for the best."

Mrs. Fowler leaned closer. "So what I've heard it true. You've been running things all by yourself the last few years."

Zillia shook her head. "Oh, no, Ma'am. I've had help from the Eckhart family, especially Soonie and Wylder. I never would have made it this far without them."

"It's truly amazing." A faraway look came into Mrs. Fowler's eyes. "The three of you, barely more than children and caring for that entire farm." She turned her focus back to Zillia. "Why not sell the land and move back into town? You and Orrie could live on the money for a while, at least."

Again, the suggestion to sell out. Too tired to go into a long explanation, Zillia shook her head. "I can't."

Orrie turned his cup over on top of his head. A few cooled

drops of cider slid down his cheek. "Zilly, let's go home."

"The flies will eat you alive on the way." Zillia wiped his face with the hem of her dress.

"I have a plan!" Mrs. Fowler rose from her stool. "It can't be easy to stay warm in that big house during the winter. My daughter moved her family to Austin a few months ago, and Charles and I haven't known what to do with our empty home. The silence is dreadful, and we miss our grandchildren."

Zillia remembered the family. A father, mother and three ruddy-faced children who sat on the second pew every Sunday. The youngest girl was the same age as Orrie.

"Why don't you come and live with us?" Mrs. Fowler continued. "We have plenty of room and toys for Orrie. For the cold season, at least."

"How would... we could never pay you..." Zillia began.

"Oh yes, you could!" Mrs. Fowler gestured for them to follow her outside. "I'm so busy with church matters and the Town Improvement Society. I barely have time to clean my own home. I would love to have someone help me tidy up the place and do some light cooking."

"I'm not the best cook."

"You have to be better than me." Mrs. Fowler clasped her gloved hands. "Oh, please come! I don't even have to ask my husband, I know he would be delighted to have a little one in the house again."

Should I agree to it? Could I possibly accept such an offer?

Orrie needed her to make good decisions for both of them. And Orrie's needs were more important than the pride burning so fiercely throughout her body. Mama would have said yes.

"Well, I'm sure Grandpa Walt and Grandma Louise would be glad to keep the animals in exchange for milk and eggs. As for our mule, Sometimes, I'll sell him to Farmer Brand, and good riddance."

"Sometimes?" Mrs. Fowler's eyebrows perked.

"Because he sometimes will, and sometimes won't."

The Pastor's wife's laughter followed them down the road.

DECEMBER 1888

9

A Place to Winter

Zillia scanned the house. Would they need anything else? Much could stay here. Definitely the beds, since the Fowler's guest rooms offered much nicer places to sleep than old cots and feather ticks. She'd packed the few articles of wearable clothing. Orrie's growing collection of wooden toys from the Eckharts would come along on the wagon. Gruff, and the goats and chickens, had gone to stay with the Eckharts for the time being.

"God, keep the house safe while we're away." A bit of sadness dripped into Zillia's heart. Though the building needed repairs, it had been her only sanctuary for twelve years. *We won't be gone forever. It's just for a few months.*

Soonie waited for her outside. "We'll miss you."

"I'll miss being here." Zillia slung a bag over the wagon's side. "But you can visit whenever you come into town. Perhaps we can plan lunches after church on Sundays. I sure won't miss the cold." She smiled. "Just think, Soonie, the Fowler's have a real bathtub!"

"It does sound nice." Soonie swung a rope over the boxes and pulled it tight. "Of course, I prefer to bathe in the river."

"Oh, Soonie, you don't really do that?"

"Not on the coldest days." Soonie's eyes danced with mischief.

Orrie stood by the fence, feeding the goats bits of hay.

Zillia patted his shoulder. "Let's go, Orrie, say goodbye to the house."

"Goodbye!" Orrie called. He followed her to the wagon and climbed in.

"I can't believe you really take baths in the river." Zillia shook her head, while the wagon rattled down the road. "We've been friends for so long, but you still surprise me sometimes."

Soonie stared down at the reins. "You might not want to know about that part of me, the Comanche girl who loves to be in the woods. You'd probably think I'm not right in the head."

Zillia stared at her. *Does she truly not see how much I respect her?* "Of course not, Soonie, I would never think that. You're my best friend. My life is so crazy, with the farm and Orrie. I get caught up in my own worries and it may not seem like I care about anything else. I'm sorry."

"It doesn't hurt my feelings," Soonie replied. "But it does surprise me how much Grandma Louise knows about my activities when she has so many other things to do. Of course, she has Grandpa Walt to help bear her burdens."

"That might be nice," Zillia blurted.

"What would be nice?"

"Well, to have a good man to share my life. Maybe we could help each other."

"You have anyone in mind?"

"No." Zillia pulled her sunbonnet down to hide her red face. "But I'm almost nineteen. In Virginia, I'd be an old maid."

"Don't forget, I'm only a month younger. I'm not old!" Soonie huffed.

"I've just been doing this for so long on my own. It would be nice to have a man to swoop in and help me, so I don't always have to figure everything out."

'Men," Soonie scoffed. "They don't always have the answers either."

Jeb's sneering face flickered into Zillia's mind. Mama had been so sure about him, the handsome stranger who rode in from the north to help his widowed sister. She didn't know he'd lost his share of the family money to gambling and bad decisions. He'd seen Mama, a wealthy woman who'd recently lost her husband, as an easy target.

"My brother is a good man." Soonie's words jolted her

thoughts.

"Wylder?" Zillia gave a short laugh. "He's my best friend, except for you. Besides, why would he want a woman who already has a small child to care for?"

Soonie's mouth dropped open. "I was teasing. You've considered this? Not that I would mind having you for a sister."

"Soonie-- how could I contemplate something that's not offered? Your brother is a wonderful friend. But I don't think he could see me as more than a pesky little girl he has to help all the time."

Soonie's slim shoulders rose up and sank back down.

She's his sister, perhaps she sees something I don't. Zillia sighed. Even if Wylder held feelings for her beyond friendship, could she return those sentiments?

They turned towards the Fowler's home, down the winding drive lined with white slatted fences. A few sleepy-looking cows grazed beneath giant oak trees.

Mrs. Fowler jumped up from her front porch swing and waved a handkerchief at them. She wore a blue calico dress and a straw bonnet Zillia recognized from the hat shop. Most pastor's wives dressed in gray or black, but Mrs. Fowler rarely stuck by tradition, to the scandal of the town. She often said God wouldn't have created colors if he didn't want people to wear them.

"Come in, dear. My husband is attending a church committee meeting, so he won't be home until later. Why don't you bring your things inside?"

Zillia held out her arms for Orrie to jump down. "Come on, let's go see our room."

She and Soonie pulled boxes out of the buckboard and followed Mrs. Fowler up the porch steps and into the house.

When they entered the foyer, Orrie chewed on his finger and stared.

Zillia fought not to do the same.

The house was not grand, by any means, but it was the nicest place she had visited since her mother's death. Blue and gold patterned paper covered the walls, and red pine floors rested under her feet. Every surface appeared bright and clean, but a closer look revealed light fingerprints on the walls, and repaired cracks in the furniture.

Mrs. Fowler followed her glances and smiled. "Some things I can't bear to wash away. I miss my grandbabies so much." She dabbed at her eyes with the hankie.

Little hands appeared over the edge of a polished end-table. Orrie pulled down a basket and put it on his head.

"Orrie, no!" Zillia dropped her box and snatched it from him. "I'm sorry, he's been doing that lately."

"Don't worry, everything in his reach is safe. I can promise it's been played with before." Mrs. Fowler led them through the hall and into the sitting room.

A fireplace filled the room with welcoming crackles. Zillia was tempted to curl up in the velvety cushions of the fainting couch and take a nap.

"Your room is here." Mrs. Fowler went through a side door.

Zillia couldn't stop a delighted gasp. The bed, covered with a cheerful quilt, was twice the size of her cot at home. Lace curtains settled over a window. Against the wall, a small bed had been prepared for Orrie, along with a wooden box overflowing with toys. Her rocking chair, which had been brought over earlier, resided by the room's fireplace.

"Will this do?" Mrs. Fowler turned to her.

"It's wonderful. Too nice for us, really. I could never complete enough housework to pay for this."

Mrs. Fowler chuckled. "Do you know how much housekeeping services cost? We're happy to have you here." She sniffed the air. "I think supper might be ready. Don't worry, the neighbor lady made us some stew, so you won't have to suffer through my cooking. Why don't you and Soonie get your things settled and then we'll eat."

"What do you think?" Zillia asked Soonie when Mrs. Fowler left the room.

"I'm so happy for you." Soonie smoothed the quilt. "You and Orrie will be much warmer here. We will all worry less."

Zillia had never considered the Eckhart family might be concerned for them. So many times during the coldest months she had stepped outside to find extra bundles of firewood left by Wylder or Grandpa Walt. *This is a burden removed from their shoulders as well.*

Zillia hugged Soonie. "Thank you for everything, dear friend."

Soonie squeezed her back. "Don't forget, it is God who made all these things possible. Because He cares for His children."

"It must be true." Zillia bowed her head. "I can't imagine this happening without His provision."

A few specks of dust settled on the mantle, just out of Zillia's reach. Standing on her toes, she swiped at them with a feather duster.

Next came the windows. The panes already sparkled like drops of dew in the sunshine, but she rubbed them down with a soft rag anyway. Through the glass she could see Pastor Fowler moving through the yard. A small shape toddled behind him.

Pastor Fowler and Orrie had become fast friends. At the middle-aged gentleman's suggestion, Orrie called him "Papa Bird." When Pastor Fowler was home during the day, chances were the little boy would be right beside him, trying to imitate whatever he was doing.

Mrs. Fowler swept into the room with an armload of packages. She piled them on the floor with a sigh. "The larger my family becomes, the more shopping I have to do for Christmas. Zillia, could you please help me carry these to the parlor?"

"Of course." Zillia gathered the paper-wrapped bundles in her arms. Though chores and cooking filled her days, the tasks were fairly simple compared to back-breaking farm work. The Fowlers treated her with respect and kindness, and Orrie was considered an adopted grandson.

However, her earnings weren't piling up as fast as she'd hoped, even with meals provided. In the spring she would have to figure out something else if she wanted to keep the land.

She whisked these thoughts from her mind. Christmas would be here in a week, and the town's holiday dance was set for this weekend at the First National Bank of Bastrop's community room. Mrs. Fowler wanted her to help decorate for the special occasion. The ladies of the Improvement Society had been creating paper chains, strings of popcorn and evergreen wreaths for weeks.

Some of the women in the church had grumbled about how pastor's wives should be humble and modest, and not partake in such worldly activities. Mrs. Fowler never paid any mind to this kind of talk. She seemed very comfortable in her practices, and Pastor Fowler didn't object in the least. He trusted his wife to make good choices in her own right.

Zillia had never met a couple who seemed to complement each other so well. Any differences must have been resolved behind closed doors, because they never argued in front of her.

After arranging the packages under the Christmas tree, Zillia went out into the garden.

Orrie held up a roly-poly bug when she approached. "Look, Zilly!" He poked at the pill-shaped, grey bug and it rolled up into a little ball. Orrie giggled.

Pastor Fowler flipped a large rock over and peered under it. "I see some fine specimens over here, Orion." He stood and brushed dirt from the knees of his trousers.

"Thank you for spending so much time with Orrie. He loves bugs and animals so much," Zillia said.

"I've always had an interest in God's creatures, and Orrie and I have pleasant times." Pastor Fowler held out a small wooden box. "See what we found today?"

Two beetles and a sleepy-looking worm snake occupied the box. Zillia stepped back. "Um– Very nice. Pastor, I had something I wanted to discuss with you. About dancing."

"Hmmm." Pastor Fowler frowned. "Though some churches have spoken about the evils of dancing, I have no objection to it. King Solomon himself said, 'There is a time to mourn, and a time to dance.' And it's good exercise."

"What if people danced for God?"

Pastor Fowler rubbed his beard and stared into the treetops. "Well, the Bible talks about dancing in the Old and New Testament. All throughout Psalms we are instructed to dance before the Lord and sing praises to him. The prophetess Miriam danced with a tambourine in Exodus. And David danced before the Lord, although I don't think we should adopt his exact method." Pastor Fowler grinned sheepishly.

"So you think God wants us to dance for Him now?"

Pastor Fowler tapped his chin. "Most girls think of nothing but fashion and husbands. I've never had a conversation like this with a young person, but I'm glad you asked. I will have to put thought and prayer into the subject, but my quick reply would be, yes, if God still wishes for songs of praise and thanksgiving, He most likely wants us to dance in the present day as well."

Would I have the courage to dance? Certainly not in front of everyone. *But maybe when it's just me and God. And Orrie. He would probably dance with me.*

When Zillia came back into the parlor, Mrs. Fowler was lighting a row of candles on the mantelpiece.

"One can never have too much light." The older woman's mouth quirked up at the corners. "So, who's taking you to the holiday dance? Or have you decided yet? I'm sure such a pretty girl would have many suitors to choose from." Her forehead wrinkled. "What about that handsome young man you're always talking to after church? Soonie's brother."

"Mrs. Fowler!" Zillia gasped. "Wylder is like family. Besides, I'm not going to the dance, I have to stay home and care for Orrie."

"Oh, that's already been arranged." Mrs. Fowler waved her hand, as if to dismiss the problem. "Mrs. Betty's arthritis has been acting up and she doesn't want to go. She'd be happy to take care of him for the evening. So you can come assist me. Of course," she grinned slyly, "I will only need your help for oh, maybe five or ten minutes? That should give you plenty of time to dance. You do know how?"

"Of course... Mama taught me. But what would I do with myself? No one's asked me, and I have nothing to wear."

"Mrs. Plummer and I were just discussing the shameful

number of unmarried young men who live in this town. I'm sure you will have a line of gentlemen waiting out the door to waltz with you. I have a lovely lavender silk dress you can borrow. The color never suited me with my pale skin and red hair, but I think it will bring out your eyes just beautifully."

"I... it sounds wonderful." In the few short weeks she had lived in the Fowler's home, she had learned not to argue with her employer when she had her mind set. The thought of an evening where she could simply feel beautiful and enjoy herself seemed as impossible as a trip to the moon.

10

The Dance

Lavender silk spilled out in graceful waves over the steps of the bank building. Zillia giggled as the enormous bustle followed behind her. Though bustles were the height of fashion, she never understood the notion to appear like a small child was hiding beneath her skirts. "I might as well have brought Orrie along," she whispered to Soonie.

Soonie's gown, though simpler than Zillia's borrowed finery, was splendid. The crushed green velvet had taken her and Grandma Louise weeks to sew. A collar of antique Swedish lace lay around her neck, and a choker of pearls shone on her tan throat. Coils of hair crowned her head, far different than the two braids she normally wore.

"Soonie, you look beautiful."

Soonie's cheeks brightened. "We both do." They swept through the door.

The hall served for town meetings, auctions and election headquarters. This evening, most of the chairs were lined up against the walls. Lanterns winked from every table and hung from hooks attached to the ceiling. Chains of colored paper and tin stars dripped from the railings, and wreaths of evergreen filled the air with a sharp, wild essence. Zillia felt as though she had stepped into a fairy ring, like Mama used to tell her about.

Cakes, cookies and sweetmeats of all kinds were piled on tables lining the walls. Crowds of men and women clustered together and sipped punch from fragile china cups, lent for the occasion by the members of the Improvement Society.

And not a Trent in sight. Jemima was out of town visiting friends for the holidays.

Several of the men fixed their eyes on Soonie, but many, Zillia realized with a start, also stared at her.

She bit her lip. *Should I have come without a partner?* Mama used to talk about balls and parties back home in Virginia, but manners and traditions were so different here.

Soonie had said Wylder would be there later in the evening. At least she'd have one dance partner. He wouldn't leave her to stand by the wall all night. *Would he?*

Mrs. Fowler sailed over to the two girls in a dazzling white lace dress. "Zillia, you look stunning! Let me see your hair."

Zillia turned her neck obediently. Her carefully arranged curls, so often tangled beyond fixing, were draped in an artful chignon.

"Soonie, you did a beautiful job," said Mrs. Fowler. "And you look very pretty as well."

Soonie's face lit up. "Thank you. The room looks lovely." She gestured around her. "I can see everyone worked very hard."

"I think it's quite nice for a little ol' river town." Mrs. Fowler straightened an evergreen wreath. She took Zillia's arm. "Would you come with me? I did have one little task, before you join in the festivities."

"Yes, ma'am." Zillia followed the bustling figure into a side room, where the air was thick with cigar smoke and male voices. She looked around for more paper chains to hang or a pile of centerpieces to arrange, but instead found herself being led to a gentleman's side.

The man, a head taller than anyone else in the room, stooped down to greet them. His starched shirt crackled under his coat. "Mrs. Fowler, so nice to see you. Who is this fetching creature?"

"Mr. Ulysses Alder, I present Zillia Bright. She's the young lady I mentioned who is staying with me for the winter. I wanted to introduce the two of you, since you are new in town." She turned to Zillia. "Mr. Alder is from North Carolina."

Mr. Alder dipped his head further, but he kept his eyes turned up so they never left Zillia's face. His thin blond moustache curved with his smile.

Almost too late, she held out a gloved hand.

He brushed it with a kiss. "A pleasure, Miss Bright."

Zillia turned to Mrs. Fowler for help, but she only caught the last hint of white lace disappearing through the side door. Flustered, she turned back to Mr. Alder.

"Cider?" Mr. Alder picked up a cup from a nearby table.

Her hands shook when she took it from him. Was she holding her cup right? She closed her eyes and tried to remember Mama's instructions. *Everyone here is so refined and genteel.* She felt like a dress from the bottom of the rag barrel.

"My time in River County has been most pleasant. Have you lived in the area for long?" Mr. Alder shortened his 'A's much like her parents had done.

"I live outside of town, normally."

"I'm sorry, I can't hear a word coming out of your pretty little mouth. Let's try over here." Mr. Alder led her to a less crowded corner of the room. He turned and nodded for her to go on.

"I have a farm. I've been here twelve years," Zillia added hastily, realizing she hadn't answered his original question. "My parents moved down from Virginia."

He put a finger up and shook his head. "It's still too loud." He held open a door for her and she went through it. They stepped out into the crisp evening air.

"Thank you for humoring me, Miss Bright. I couldn't hear myself think in there. And the heat." Mr. Alder fanned himself with his hat. "Northern winters are much colder and I'm afraid I came dressed for a blizzard."

"It's been awhile, but I do remember those days,' Zillia replied. "We'd have had a foot of snow in Virginia by now. In Texas, we might get a dusting. I'm sure many people here can't abide harsh winters." She stared out at the pools of light spilling out into the street from windows. "But I do miss snow, sometimes."

Mr. Alder's eyes didn't leave her face, but he said nothing.

She fumbled for something to say. "What brings you to this strange and warm land?"

He leaned back on the porch rail. "My father's friend invited me to join his law firm. I passed the bar last spring. The town has grown so much, he hasn't been able to keep up with business."

"The bar exam? What a challenge that must have been."

He chuckled. "Yes, it certainly was. But I pulled through, and here I am."

The unseasonably warm air caused her hands to sweat, so without thinking she pulled off her gloves and waved her fingers in the air to dry.

Mr. Alder stared at her hands. "Your skin is so rough. What on earth did you do--"

"I told you I lived on a farm," Zillia jammed her fingers back into her glove. She lifted her chin and moved towards the door.

"Of course, of course," Mr. Alder stammered. "That was terribly rude of me." He touched her elbow. "Please accept my apology. I just-- have so much to learn about Texas ladies."

Zillia lowered her eyes.

"Miss Bright, could you possibly forgive me enough to allow me a dance?"

Flashes of color passed by the window and strains of music floated through the double doors. Now Zillia understood the patient hours her mother had spent teaching her to dance in their country kitchen. She'd felt quite silly at the time, surrounded by dirty dishes and chopped vegetables. Now here she was, Zillia Bright, asked to dance by a true gentleman.

"Of course I will." Zillia offered her hand, and Mr. Alder pulled her into the flurry of laughter and warmth.

Zillia tried to hold her hand steady while he took it into his own. She kept a bit of distance while they turned and swayed, praying he couldn't feel her trembling. She'd never danced with a man before, except for Papa.

Mr. Alder proved to be a fine dancer, and either didn't notice or ignored her nervousness. "I think I'll stay in Texas for a while," he said, as they spun beneath the room's one chandelier.

Zillia relaxed, and a wave of joy warmed her soul. *How wonderful to have no responsibility or duties, just for a short time.*

After two dances they were both too warm to continue. They sank against a wall, laughing.

"You dance very well," Mr. Alder said.

Paper fans lay on the tables for general use, and Zillia picked one up and fluttered it before her face. "For a farm girl, you mean?"

"Of course not." Mr. Alder's light brows drew together. "I

mean, you're a wonderful dancer. I quite enjoyed myself."

"Well, thank you." Zillia's cheeks were warm, and not because of the room. *Why do I always say the wrong thing?* He could have spent the evening with any woman at the party, he certainly had his choice. This man was obviously trying to be kind and not patronizing. *I have no business being in this place where only proper ladies belong.* Her fancy gown suddenly felt like peacock's plumage. She longed for her broad-brimmed hat and papa's old coat.

"Are you all right?" He searched her eyes.

"I'm fine," she answered, though really, she wasn't.

The waltz ended. Zillia spotted Soonie across the room. Her friend's cheeks were rosy as she swept her partner a graceful curtsy.

Zillia was about to weave through the crowd to her friend when she heard boots thump, and a jingle of spurs. Only one man in town would wear spurs to a dance. Abel Trent swaggered through the door. He slammed it behind him, knocking over a row of men's walking sticks that leaned against the wall. Wrinkles covered his suit and his tie hung askew. His eyes were fixed on Soonie.

Zillia hastened to reach her friend first, to warn or shield her somehow, but the heavy skirts tripped her and she fell against a chair.

Soonie's bright, happy eyes filled with dismay when Abel's meaty fingers sank into her velvet sleeve. "Can I help you, Mr.

Trent?" She jerked away from his grasp.

"Don't need no help from a half-breed," Abel Trent wheezed and grabbed for her arm again. "Just wanted a dance." The giant man pulled Soonie out into the middle of the floor. "Come on, music makers," he bellowed. "Let's have another waltz!"

Soonie stood stiffly, her eyes dark and dangerous now. "I do not wish to dance with you."

Zillia bit her lip until she tasted blood. *Is anyone going to stop him?*

Her eyes lit on one of the walking sticks. Thick and twisted, with a round brass top. Her fingers closed around the cane and she drew it up so it was hidden in the folds of her skirt.

She moved through the gaping onlookers and was only a few lengths away from Soonie's side when a tall figure in a white shirt stepped in front of her.

"I'll deal with this, Zillia." Wylder said.

In one quick movement Soonie was whisked out of the way, and before Abel could react he found himself facing her older brother.

"You heard my sister," Wylder said. "She doesn't want to dance with you."

The crowd pressed against the edges of the room and a few ladies began to thread out through the doors. Zillia couldn't help but think of Mrs. Fowler and how sad she would be about her dance being spoiled. That Abel Trent! She clutched her cane and moved closer to hear what was being said by the two glaring young men.

Abel Trent leaned into Wylder's face. "I oughta– you know, I oughta–."

"What, Abel?" came a voice from the door. Sheriff Williams strode over to the center of the room. "I recollect this young feller beatin' you in a fair fight, more n' once. Be a shame to bother the doctor for stitches this late at night."

By the look in Wylder's eye Zillia was sure he'd be happy to give the doctor more business, but he moved out of the sheriff's way and stood by Soonie.

Abel relaxed and stepped backwards, raising his hands in front of him. "Never mind, never mind. Not like she's worth nothin' anyway." He staggered towards the door.

"No, you're not going out to make anyone else miserable tonight, Abel Trent." The sheriff grabbed his arm. "We'll just allow you to visit your regular cell so you can sober up." He pulled the swearing Abel outside and shut the door.

A collective sigh ran through the building. Couples moved back out on the floor while the music started again.

Zillia set the cane back against the wall and hurried to Soonie. "Are you all right?"

Her friend pulled out a handkerchief and dabbed a few beads of sweat off her nose. "It's a good thing Wylder arrived, I'm not sure if it would have been ladylike to murder, and anyway, it's against the Ten Commandments."

Wylder came back with a glass of punch for his sister. "Glad I came in when I did. I can't believe the whole town was going to stand there and let that man bully you."

"Don't be too upset." Soonie smoothed her collar. "They'd hardly had any time to react. And you know as well as I do some towns wouldn't have even let us attend a public function."

Soonie's used to this. She deals with rejection every day, if only from people's eyes or gestures. A new respect flooded Zillia's heart. Until Mama married Jeb, she had never experienced people thinking badly of her for reasons beyond her control.

The music started up, and soon couples were spinning out on the floor. Wylder turned to Zillia, his eyes shining in the lantern light. "May I have this dance?"

A mixture of emotions buzzed around Zillia's stomach like a hive of bees. "Thank you for asking, but not presently. Mrs. Fowler is probably at her wit's end, and I really should check on her."

Fingers rested on her elbow. She glanced up to see Mr. Alder. "If I may, Ma'am. Mrs. Fowler left a few moments ago."

"Oh dear! Yes, I'd better go home." Zillia turned to Wylder, who was giving the young lawyer a quizzical look. "Wylder, this is Mr. Ulysses Alder. Mr. Alder, my friend, Mr. Wylder Eckhart."

The two men bowed awkwardly.

"Wylder, please save my dance for another time." Zillia smiled in apology.

"May I walk you home?" both men asked at the same time.

A situation Zillia had never dreamed she'd encounter. Her

head spun. What should she do? *Wylder is my friend, surely he would understand me not wanting to offend a newcomer.* She reached for Mr. Alder's hand. "Wylder, thank you for the offer."

"I'll see you tomorrow at church," she said to Soonie.

While the young lawyer guided her to the door, Wylder's eyes filled with hurt and confusion. Zillia stepped out into the night wondering if she had made a terrible mistake.

APRIL 1889

11

River Elves

"Elves! Elves at the river!"

Zillia put down her milking pail and walked to the edge of the bluff.

Orrie ran up to meet her. Dirt smudged his cheeks and snail shells dotted the path behind him where he had dropped them in his haste.

"Elves? Surely not." *Maybe I should stop reading him tales from my old fairy book.* "Let's get the lantern, it's getting too dark to see down there. Perhaps you can show me the elves."

Zillia tugged her brother up the bank to the house. She took the lantern from its hook on the porch and they headed back down the hill.

The river was swollen after the early spring rains. Moonlight danced on the water while it swirled around tiny rock and branch islands. Early wildflowers filled the air with their powdery sweet scent. Thick, throaty sounds echoed from the muddy shallows and rocks.

With one hand, Zillia held Orrie back from the water, and with the other, she lowered the lantern.

A sleek, green shape hopped away from the light, and then another.

"See, Zillia, elves!"

A laugh escaped her lips. "No Orrie, those are frogs! Mama used to call them peepers. Just watch."

The two of them crouched down by the ground. Zillia could feel Orrie quivering in excitement.

Another frog hopped in front of them. Its throat ballooned out and released an unearthly croak into the night.

"See, Orrie, that's how they talk," Zillia whispered. These moments were the best part of caring for her brother, the times she could share something new and watch his eyes shine in wonder.

When all the frogs had disappeared, Zillia sat on a log and pulled Orrie onto her lap. "The stars sure are pretty tonight. See those three in a row? That's Orion's belt. My papa always said he was the hunter of the skies." Zillia took her brother's chubby finger in her hand and held it up to each star, tracing the shape of the mythical hero. "There's his belt, and his bow. He's strong and brave, just like I knew you would be. That's why I named you after him."

"Yep, I'm brave." Orrie wriggled down to the ground. The lantern light played on features to reveal his face was changing again. Every day he left behind another baby trait and became more of a little person.

"Well, it's time all the brave heroes went to bed."

They walked back up to the house. Zillia had to admit she missed the open land and the country quiet. Sometimes she'd allow herself a moment to listen to the river sing.

A week had passed since they had returned from town. Wylder had not come by, but she wasn't surprised. He'd be busy with spring planting.

A silence had sprung up between Zillia and Wylder since the dance. She gave it little thought the first few Sundays, when he barely tipped his hat or gave a mumbled "good morning." After a few weeks, she knew something was wrong. By then, she felt too awkward to bring it up.

Mr. Alder had come by to visit her a few times at the Fowler's. He'd made his intentions clear, but she could do nothing to encourage his advances. No fluttery feelings entered her heart when she saw him come up the drive, even though he was quite handsome. Yes, he could offer an escape from this life, but she had seen Mama throw her life away for a loveless marriage and she wasn't about to make that choice.

They reached an unspoken agreement to remain friends.

Saying goodbye to the Fowlers had been tough for everyone, especially Mr. Fowler, who kept blowing his nose in his silken handkerchief. But Zillia knew they couldn't stay there if she wanted to keep up with the farm.

Returning to the farm was even stranger with Grandpa Walt coming in Wylder's place. She missed her friend's warm smile and his encouraging words.

The lantern light winked along the path as she led Orrie back to the house. He stumbled sleepily beside her, humming a tune she recognized as one of the lullabies she often sang.

Orrie was quickly snuggled into his little bed and on his way to dreamland. His gentle snores drifted from underneath his quilt.

Gruff sank down at the foot of Orrie's bed with a contented sigh. Once settled, he would not leave his little master's side.

With her small charge down for the night, thoughts began to swirl through Zillia's head. *What will I do about the crops this year? Why is Wylder so upset with me?* She stepped back outside to ponder them in the cool evening air.

The song of the peepers was the perfect background music for her wonderings. Her favorite rock gleamed in the moonlight at the edge of the clearing. She scooted across the stone until she settled into a comfortable place and tucked her knees under her chin.

The house, though a bit musty, had seemed to welcome them. Accommodating as the Fowlers had been, it was nice to settle back into their own space and routine. Even the chickens and goats seemed happy to return to their own pens and yard.

But what am I going to do now? She'd never be able to keep things going without money. She buried her face in the folds of her apron.

"Papa, I've tried so hard," she sobbed. "I don't see how I can do it this time. I'm going to have to sell the farm."

A loud crack from the brush answered her, followed by more snapping. A man grunted.

One hand rubbed away her tears while the other scrabbled through the dirt beside the rock until she found a branch the thickness of her wrist. Who could it be? A drifter? A lone Comanche scout? She never came outside without a gun. Only tonight.

Rising as silently as she could, she gripped her stick and crept along the path. The crash had come from her left and though every instinct screamed for her to run, she had to protect Orrie.

The broad-shouldered man's face was shadowed as he rose to his feet.

Zillia brought the stick high over her head.

The man turned a second before wood contacted skull, grabbing the branch. "Zillia, what are you doing?" Wylder yelled.

"I could ask you the same thing! Wylder Eckhart, you gave me the biggest fright of my life! Why on earth are you out here? I almost knocked you senseless."

His eyes twinkled in the lantern light. "You were really going to hit me, weren't you? Do you think you could have knocked me out with that piece of kindling? What if I had been someone with evil intentions?"

"I could have dealt with it." She raised her chin. "I've been out here for a while, and I reckon I've learned how to take care of myself."

"Is that so?" Wylder tipped his head back and folded his arms across his chest. "You think this is the first time I've come out here to check on you?"

Suddenly, missing pieces of a puzzle clicked together in Zillia's mind. Wylder's red eyes, the times he fell asleep in church, the days he couldn't stop yawning. She always assumed it was from when he'd stay up too late carving by the fire, or because of working so hard. Would she have guessed he came late at night to spy on her? *Never.*

Her heart beat faster. How many of her whispered conversations with God had he overheard? Over the years on her rock, she had created a spoken journal of ideas and dreams. Sometimes she had even sung them. It was as though Wylder had trespassed in her thoughts.

Fingernails dug into her palms as she glared at him. "I never asked for your help." She knew how ungrateful these words sounded after the years of work and support he had given without a dime paid back. "You have no right to come out here and spy on me!"

"That's not why I came, and you know it, Zillia," he was shouting now, something he never did unless he was trying to communicate across a barn or a cornfield. "You're crazy, you know that? Trying to run this farm by yourself and take care of everything. It's not safe!"

"You said I was doing a good job!"

"Yes." His voice softened. "But that's when I could be here to help out, to keep watch. I'll be gone soon, and I won't..."

"Fine with me, leave." The words felt like ice on her lips, and for a moment she thought someone else was speaking them. "I can take care of myself."

"No, you won't," he said slowly. "You'll just find someone else. Maybe that lawyer. He'd do a better job anyway, right?" He stepped back, and his jaw tightened. "At least he has money. He'll buy you whatever you want."

Now she was confused. "Ulysses Alder? He is going to help me try to get the deed for the land in my name. I really don't understand why you're so upset about him. He's just a friend."

"He'd better stay away from me," Wylder muttered, and pulled his hat down further over his eyes.

A tremor washed over her and she turned away from him, folding her arms around her body against the shiver. "I think you should leave, Mr. Eckhart. And there's no need for you to come back."

"Wait, Zillia." His voice broke. "I'm sorry. I scared you, I didn't mean to..."

She walked up the bank, across the yard and into the house, where she slammed the door in his face.

MAY 1889

12

Meeting Uncle Isak

"Why is my brother angry with you?"

Zillia gripped the buckboard's seat tighter. She had tried to avoid the topic for the last few days, but she knew her blunt friend wouldn't leave it alone forever. "Didn't he tell you what happened?"

"Just because Wylder is my brother doesn't mean he shares everything." Soonie shrugged. "I noticed he's been upset since the dance. He looked especially gloomy after he made his rounds out at your house the other night."

Zillia gasped. "You mean, you knew he'd been coming out this entire time?"

"Of course I did. Grandpa wouldn't have allowed you to stay out there on your own without someone checking up on you."

"So it was Grandpa Walt who sent him out?" Zillia rubbed her forehead.

Soonie nodded. "At first he planned to ask the hired man to go. Wylder volunteered to ride out every few nights. He's been doing it for years, except when you stayed with the Fowlers."

Zillia sank back against the seat. "How did I never see him?" *And I thought I was doing such a good job keeping watch.* "I wish someone had told me."

One of Soonie's dark eyebrows arched up. "Do you?"

"Yes. Well, I don't know," Zillia faltered. *Would I have wanted to know he lost so much sleep because of me?*

She leaned forward on the wagon seat, straining to see further down the road. "How long does this trip usually take?"

"A few hours. I'm so glad you and Orrie came with me today; it makes the time go faster."

Every year, Soonie's relatives from North Texas brought goods to a town outside of Austin. Soonie's uncle always came a little farther south after the trade days to swap items and visit.

Usually Wylder and Soonie went together, but this year Soonie asked Zillia to come along. She thought her uncle would give a good price for the bushels of pecans Zillia had hoarded in the barn.

The gardens were planted, the paltry amount of corn had been sown, and a few loose boards on the chicken shed had been repaired. So Zillia allowed herself the rare treat of a day's outing.

The horses clomped across the dock to the ferry station. Soonie hopped down from the wagon. "Orrie, you want to help?"

Orrie nodded and climbed out. "Can I pull, Soonie?"

With a boost from Soonie, he was able to reach the worn, thick rope attached to the signal bell. One good tug, and the bell swayed wildly, tolling out across the river.

Soonie held Orrie's hand on the dock while Zillia stayed in the wagon, holding the reins.

"Wonder where Mr. Teller is." Soonie squinted at the ferry man's station across the river.

"Who knows," Zillia replied. The ferry man was notorious for wandering off to go fishing. Complaints had been made for years, but no one else was willing to take the job.

Finally, a man wearing overalls appeared at the door of the small hut across the river. He stared out at the party on the dock, shook his head, and made his way over to the ferry.

Orrie loved the ferry ride. "Fishies!" he shouted as several silvery shapes darted under the wide, wooden platform.

"Stay close to me, you little rascal." Zillia pulled him back from the edge.

After crossing the river, Soonie directed the horses down the wide, twisting road towards Austin. After a while, they stopped beside a small pond for lunch. A blanket of nodding bluebonnets and Indian Paintbrushes spread out before them.

Orrie bit into a biscuit and grinned. "This is good. When will we be there?"

"Just another hour or so." Soonie pointed up to the sky. "See, the sun is over there. When it gets to that spot, we'll be at the place."

"That's forever and ever, Soonie!" Orrie pouted.

"Perhaps we can make the drive seem shorter if we discuss the cookies I have for a certain boy at the end of the trip." Soonie reached over to tickle him.

He fell over in the grass, laughing. "Hey." He sat back up. "Soonie, are the cookies for me?"

Soonie smiled over his head at Zillia. "Your cookies? Oh, I thought they were for some other little boy."

Though still early in the spring, the sun was blazing by the time they arrived. The horses' flanks were drenched in sweat and drool dripped from their bits.

A small cluster of homes gathered around the big trading post building, like chicks huddled around a mother hen. The trading post served as a store, meeting place, watering hole and post office for wagons traveling from Austin to River County.

A man sat in the shade of the building's wall, his eyes shut tight.

"There's Uncle Isak." Soonie pulled back on the reigns.

Though half white, Isak had chosen to fully embrace the Comanche lifestyle. His hair hung in two long braids, like Soonie's. As the wagon approached, his eyes flew open, shining like turquoise beads in his tanned face.

"Soonie, maruawe." Isak held out a hand to help her down. "It's good to see you, Little One. I am sorry Wylder, Henry and Will could not come."

"They and Grandpa and Grandma send their love." Soonie smiled. She gestured to Zillia. "This is my friend, Zillia Bright."

Isak bowed his head. "Thank you for coming. Travelers in groups are always safest."

"So, what did you bring to trade?" Soonie's eyes danced.

"You will have to come see. My pack is over this way." Isak turned and walked to side of the building.

Orrie bounced in the back of the wagon. "Let me out, Zilly!"

"I'm going to take Orrie for a walk," Zillia told Soonie. "We'll be back in a few minutes." Her part of the bartering could wait.

Orrie skipped ahead of her into an expansive meadow spread out behind the little town. Hills rose in gentle green slopes, dotted with flowers of all colors and shapes. Sunk in the middle, like a button sewn into a cushion, rested a little pond.

Cattails surrounded the small body of water. Zillia plucked a sausage-like stem and held it out to Orrie. "Look, when you pull this apart, it's all soft."

He patted the fluff for a moment, then dropped the stalk and moved toward the water. "Look! Fishies and froggies!"

Zillia rolled her eyes and grabbed his hand as he leaned over to get a closer look. She should have known he'd be more interested in the fauna than the flora. His bare feet sank into the thick mud.

"Let's not get too dirty." She pulled him back to dry ground. Soonie wouldn't appreciate muddy toes on her newly acquired goods.

After her little brother had examined every bug, turtle and frog the small body of water had to offer, Zillia decided to take him back to the post and check on Soonie.

Niece and uncle leaned against the wagon, talking in low, earnest voices. They turned when she approached.

"Come and see what you want to trade," said Isak. He led them over to his packs, stacked on the ground for the afternoon to give his mule a break.

Zillia eyed the colorful baskets and beaded jewelry. *Such beautiful things.* She touched a bright blanket. "How much for this one?"

"How many pecans do you have?" Isak arched an eyebrow.

"Two bushels."

He pulled out three blankets and placed them in her arms. "Is this a good trade?"

"It seems like too much," Zillia said.

Isak shook his head. "We don't have pecans near the reservation. Everyone will enjoy the change."

"Well, thank you." Zillia traced an intricate pattern in awe. She would never have the patience to create something so lovely, even if she had the time.

They spread out one of the blankets under a tree and talked for a while longer.

Isak spoke of the turmoil within the Comanche people. "Some just want to live in peace. Others take whatever they can, while they can."

War parties still sprang up in the south from time to time. Sometimes Zillia forgot about these troubles, wrapped up in her own difficulties. Many good people had lost their lives, on both sides.

Soonie's lips trembled while she listened to her uncle, and tears glistened in her eyes.

Zillia reached out to squeeze her hand. *Soonie never forgets.*

After a short time, Isak rose to his feet. "I must go, Soonie. Take care of yourself, and the little boys." He hugged his niece. "Please think about what I asked."

Soonie nodded. "May God ride with you, Uncle."

A few moments after they started for home, Orrie wrapped himself in colorful blankets and fell asleep.

"What was Isak talking to you about while we were gone?" Zillia asked.

"Hmmm." Soonie's eyes narrowed. "He wants me to come to the reservation. I always got high grades in school, and he thinks I could be a good teacher. Some of the children don't even know how to read."

"You would be perfect!" Zillia clapped her hands. "Oh, Soonie, what a wonderful opportunity for you." She stopped when she saw the wistful smile tugging at the corner of her friend's mouth. "Of course, I would miss you."

"Yes, it would be hard to leave," said Soonie. "But the boys are getting older and will be more help to Grandma and Grandpa. My heart has always been with my people."

"I know." But Zillia couldn't imagine life without her friend.

"I'll be going to work with Wylder next month," Soonie said suddenly.

"They allow women to chop the lumber?" Zillia had never heard of such a thing.

"No. Even though I could do just as well," Soonie scowled. "I'm going to join a few other women who will be cooking for them. It's a big project and should last at least a month. I'll be taking the train a week after Wylder leaves. It's good money."

"Don't those camps usually have men cooks?" asked Zillia.

Soonie nodded. "But this camp threw out three already. The crew threatened to leave if they didn't find someone who could make better food. So I suppose they decided to try something new."

Zillia stroked the sleeping Orrie's cheek. "I wish I could go, but what would I do with him?"

"Didn't Mrs. Fowler offer to care for him any time? You could come back on the weekends. The train will be hauling loads of lumber every Monday and Friday."

"It would be hard to leave him, but I'd make more money than the corn would bring in. Maybe I could find someone to live out on the farm for a while in exchange for vegetables, eggs and such. I'll consider the idea," Zillia promised.

The rest of the trip was made in silence, with the boy sleeping between them all the way back to the ferry and home.

JUNE 1889

13

The Lumber Camp

"We don't normally take passengers, especially womenfolk." The conductor removed his cap and mopped his shiny, bald head with a handkerchief. "But no other train is going towards the camp for two more weeks, and the foreman's in bad need of camp cooks." He helped Zillia into the dark boxcar and handed up her small bag. She and Soonie found places to settle among the piles of boxes and barrels.

The conductor leaned inside and peered at them in the half-light. "You all settled?"

"Yes, sir," Soonie said.

The wide panel closed, and they were left in darkness.

Zillia's eyes gradually picked out the small creases of light from cracks in the board.

A whistle pierced the boxcar. Smoke drifted into the enclosure, the soot cutting through the musty car and burning her nose. It made her head ache. The train lurched beneath them.

This was the first time Zillia had ridden a train since she and her parents had come from Virginia, so long ago. A familiar wave of nausea hit her. She had spent most of the trip, which had lasted for several days, with her head resting in Mama's lap. Mama had stroked her hair and whispered, "You'll be all right, Zilly, girl."

"I wish we had windows, at least," Soonie murmured in the darkness beside her.

Zillia closed her eyes and leaned against a burlap bag. She wouldn't have dared to watch the blur of trees and houses, even if she could have seen them. Just the thought made her stomach lurch.

Soonie pinched her hand. "You miss Orrie?"

"Not yet. Right now the only thing I can think to miss is solid ground beneath my feet."

"We're going to take this journey every Friday afternoon and Monday morning," Soonie reminded her. "I hope you get used to it. It would take much longer by wagon."

"I know." Zillia wiped her sweat-drenched face with her apron. "But I don't get sick riding in a wagon."

"True."

The other two women, Mrs. Williams and Mrs. Dawson, had been allowed to ride with the train operators in a front car. Zillia would have liked the opportunity to chat with them along the way, but at the same time, she didn't know how much conversation she could have managed.

"The men have been out there for a month with dismal cooks. How have they survived this long?" She untied her sunbonnet, pulled it off, and began to fan her face.

"Goodness knows." Soonie wriggled around beside her, pushing crates and barrels to the side. "Probably just ate salt pork straight from a barrel. I'm sure they'll be glad to see us."

"I overheard Pastor. Fowler and Grandpa Walt talking to the other women. They told them to watch us with 'gimlet eyes.' Like we can't take care of ourselves."

"We've been the talk of the town since we decided to come. Everyone was scandalized," replied Soonie.

Mrs. Purpose had whispered to Zillia after church. "Wild men work at those lumber camps. It's not a proper place for a young lady, not proper at all."

What would Mrs. Purpose have thought if she'd seen her watching for varmints at the farm in Papa's coat and hat, baby strapped to her back, riding a mule with a hundred year old shotgun across her lap? Her record was three coyotes in one night. Mrs. Purpose probably never saw even one wild pig.

"Thank you," she had said to the old woman, whose skin wrinkled with worry under her ostrich-plumed straw wonder.

"Soonie and I will be all right. Mr. Eckhart will be there, along with several men from town. They'll take care of us."

Mrs. Purpose hadn't replied, just pursed her lips like she'd bitten into something sour. She'd bustled off muttering about 'girls without mothers.'

The train shuddered to a halt. Zillia didn't realize she had dozed off until she touched her face and felt impressions the boards had left on her skin.

Soonie nudged her. "Feeling better?"

"I suppose." Zillia rubbed her eyes and yawned. "Are we there?"

"I think so. No way to tell until they open the door."

The door slid open in response. Mr. Calbott, the conductor, peered in at them. "You ladies handle the trip all right?"

"We're fine." Soonie stood and held out her hand to Zillia.

Zillia pulled herself up and swayed a little as she picked her way to the door. She smoothed the wrinkles out of her new traveling suit which had been a Christmas present from Mrs. Fowler.

Now she missed Orrie. Doubts began to creep into her mind. She had never spent more than one night away from her brother. The Fowlers were delighted to have him back and he was in good hands. Would he cry in the night because she wasn't there? No one could reach her if something happened; the train only went through twice a week. Her thoughts raced as she stood at the boxcar door. *What can I do?*

"Miss Bright?" Wylder stood outside of the train car. His eyes glittered in a look normally reserved for strangers.

Soonie must not have told him I was coming. His hair had grown out since she had seen him at church six weeks ago. Dark curls fell to his collar. His beard was thick and dark, not the trim goatee he usually sported.

Soonie hugged him. "I'm so happy! I wasn't expecting you here."

Wylder returned the hug. "They sent me with the wagon to fetch you ladies, and the supplies."

He held out a stiff hand to Zillia. "Allow me to help you down, Miss Bright." his voice was frosty as January.

"You certainly may." Zillia replied in a voice just as cold. She took his hand and stepped to the train platform, which had been fashioned from wooden boxes.

"If you will excuse me, I'm off to tend to the supplies." He nodded toward the men unloading.

"Of course. Thank you Wyld..." She caught herself. "Mr. Eckhart."

She picked up her carpet bag and went to join the two older women, who stood by the wagon.

Soonie talked with Wylder while he helped unload. They were smiling and laughing. *I would be over there with them, if we hadn't quarreled.* "Oh, I hate this," she muttered.

"Dearie, it's not so bad." Plump fingers patted her hand. Mrs. Dawson's moon-shaped face, made rounder by her smiles, peered under her bonnet. "We were promised our own quarters and a kitchen, and May has been rather nice this year."

Mrs. Williams, a tall, thin woman with a beak of a nose, didn't say anything. She looked as gloomy as Zillia felt.

Nothing would have persuaded Zillia to share the truth behind her mood, so she shrugged her shoulders and climbed into the back of the large, covered wagon.

The trip to camp was mercifully short, though the wagon bumped and banged over the half-finished road. Magnificent loblolly pines stretched up into the sky on all sides of them, like a mythical forest. In the distance, shouts and crashes could be heard from the crew as they harvested the silent giants.

When they reached the camp, all was deserted. Canvas tents clustered together on one side of the clearing, and fire pits ringed a larger cooking pot suspended from a metal hook. A small tent sagged by itself in its own area.

The women climbed down from the wagon and went to inspect the tent.

"It's hardly big enough for sardines!" wailed Mrs. Williams, the first words Zillia had heard her speak all day.

"We'll make it do." Mrs. Dawson smoothed out the canvas sides. "Perhaps we can expand the walls, somehow."

"Make it do?" Mrs. Williams snapped. Scarlet spotted each thin cheek and bright tears appeared in her eyes. "We can't stay in this place. And where are we supposed to cook?" She pointed to the fire pit. "Do they expect us to live like savages?" She stepped outside the tent. "Young man!" she screeched. "Young man, come here this instant!"

"Yes, ma'am?" Wylder came over and folded his arms.

"I demand to speak to your foreman. We have been pressed, dare I say, begged, to come to this..." the woman looked around, "Bohemian forest, and we expect to be treated with respect. We are, after all, ladies."

"Of course." Wylder's lips twitched while he nodded. "I'll see if Mr. Humphreys can be spared."

"Make it quick, young man."

"Yes, ma'am." When Wylder turned to go, Zillia caught him exchanging an amused look with Soonie. Her heart jolted with an unexpected pang of sorrow. Glances of that nature would normally be shared with both of them.

She and Soonie pulled boxes and bags out of the wagon, stacking them with a few other boxes of supplies already there.

"Don't most lumber camps have bunkhouses?" Soonie asked Wylder when he returned. "We were told things would be more civilized."

"The foreman must've stretched the truth a little." Wylder stared down at the crate he'd just unpacked. "The company only wants us in this area for six more weeks. They didn't think it'd be worth the effort to build cabins. I kind of wondered why you wanted to come out here, Soonie."

Soonie's jaw set in that determined look Zillia knew so well. "I'm sure we can figure this out."

"Let's see what we have to work with." Zillia spread a piece of burlap on the ground to keep out the worst of the sand, then shoved two wooden boxes together. "We can use this for a table, for now anyway."

Mrs. Dawson came over and began unpacking containers, examining labels as she went. "Beans, salt pork, and corn meal. I suggest we plan the menu for next week, perhaps, ladies?"

Mrs. Williams frowned over her shoulder. "Next week? I won't be returning next week and if you had any sense, neither would you!"

"Ladies, welcome to our camp," a deep voice with an East Texas accent spoke behind them.

Mr. Humphries was just the sort of man Zillia had been expecting. He was short, with arms like thick oak logs, wild hair that stood on end with bits of wood chips and leaves stuck in the curls, and wrinkled clothes stained with mud. He smelled like earth and logs and sweat.

How does Wylder always smell good? Even after he's been slopping hogs.

Mrs. Williams pulled a lace-trimmed handkerchief out of her valise, held it over her nose, and glared at the foreman from behind the cloth. "This camp might be fine for a gang of hooligans, but it is no place for ladies of good breeding! We were promised comfortable and discreet quarters, and a full, functional kitchen. Not a fire-pit."

Mr. Humphries's mouth drooped under his thick walrus

moustache.

"Yes... err...Mrs."

"Mrs. Williams."

"Yes. Well, we were gonna have a kitchen all set to rights by now, and a lean-to for you ladies. But the crews ain't been gettin' here fast enough, and trees don't cut themselves. We've a sight to catch up on ma'am, and my boss don't like excuses."

When Mrs. Williams drew herself to her full height, she was over a head taller than the stocky foreman. "Neither do I. Young man," she turned to Wylder. "We expect to be taken back to the train station this instant."

"That's purty near impossible," said Mr. Humphries. "That train's headed on to Houston, and won't be back until Friday."

The bristle went out of Ms. William's shoulders and she sank down onto a crate.

"We're stuck here." She put her face in her hands. "For five entire days!"

"There, there." Mrs. Dawson patted her shoulder. "We'll figure something out."

While the two older women consoled each other, Zillia helped Soonie take inventory and sort out the few dishes they had been given.

"What supplies have you been using?" Zillia asked Mr. Humphries.

"Those, yonder." He pointed to a pile of tin containers, covered in food and buzzing with flies.

"Lovely." Soonie grabbed a bucket. "I guess I'll be taking these down to the stream, Zillia. We don't have time to boil water to wash them, so I'll use sand."

"Right. I'll get the fire stirred up."

Mr. Humphries clapped a dirty hand to Wylder's shoulder. "Time we got back to work."

"Yes, Sir." Wylder tipped his hat. "See you at lunch, ladies." The men disappeared into the trees.

Back at the largest fire pit, Zillia found a long stick and raked the coals. The large cast-iron pot hanging from the hook looked clean enough, at least, and so did the three Dutch ovens of varying sizes.

"I've made do with less," said Mrs. Dawson, while she knelt beside her.

"Me too." Zillia hauled a bucket of water from the large barrel and poured it in. "But never to cook a meal for thirty hungry men. Harvest crews on our farm never had more than ten."

"How much different can it be? Throw in a few extra handfuls of this and that." Mrs. Dawson smiled.

The woman's positive attitude was contagious, and soon she and Zillia were talking and laughing like old friends. By the time Soonie returned with a basket filled with clean stacks of cups and plates, a pot of beans soaked by the fire and corn bread was baking in a Dutch oven, buried beneath the coals.

"We don't have time for the beans to soak and cook before lunch." Zillia pointed at the sun. "We'll have to think of something else."

"Biscuits and gravy? Do you think that will suit them?" Mrs. Dawson held up a bag of flour.

"Serves them right if it doesn't," Mrs. Williams sniffed. "No one has given us instruction about anything, except to "come and cook."

A vat of gravy was prepared and dozens of biscuits baked and cooled by the time crashes in the brush announced the men's arrival.

"They sound like a herd of buffalo," Mrs. Williams whispered to Zillia.

Zillia sincerely doubted Mrs. Williams had ever been near a gathering of such beasts, but she said nothing.

The men came and sat on whatever stumps and rocks they could find. All wore thick, brightly colored jackets. At first they joked and guffawed, but sobered when they saw the women. Many of them removed their hats and dipped their heads. Zillia recognized several men from town, including Abel Trent and his brother, Harold.

The men cheered while the women passed out plates of biscuits and ladled out gravy.

"So nice to have a hot, cooked meal," said a thin man with a gray moustache. "Thank you, pretty lady." He winked at Zillia.

Wylder, who sat only a few rocks down from the man, saw the wink and glared.

Please don't say anything. Zillia begged silently.

Wylder started on a biscuit, scowling between bites.

Zillia moved on to serve the others.

After every man had eaten his fill, Mr. Humphries came to speak to the ladies. "I know our set-up ain't much right now. We already got a clearing ready and logs set aside. Shouldn't take too long."

Mrs. Williams shook leaves and twigs from her apron. "If it's almost ready, Mr. Humphries, then why isn't it complete?"

Mr. Humphries mumbled something Zillia couldn't understand and walked away.

"Hmph." Mrs. Williams gathered dirty dishes.

While men stood to return to work, Wylder came over to Soonie. "Be careful. We've found many snakes where we've been working."

Zillia's shoulders sank. Wylder cared for her safety too, she knew that, but she missed their easy friendship, more than she could express even to herself. With all her heart she wished she could take back angry words spoken in haste. *I have to apologize, but how? He still seems so angry.*

As if to support this notion, he caught her eye, frowned and looked away.

She scurried over to Mrs. Dawson and picked up the basket of dirty dishes. "I'll wash these in the water we boiled."

In a moment, Soonie joined her with the larger cooking pots, and they washed in companionable silence, the way they had worked together through hundreds of chores and farm tasks over the years. Zillia appreciated that about Soonie. She enjoyed conversation, but they also allowed each other time for their own thoughts.

This was not the case with Mrs. Dawson. She prattled on all day, speculating about the weather, repeating town gossip, wondering what funerals and weddings they might miss. Hours and hours of words tripped over themselves to find homes in the ears of her captive audience.

"She probably spends a lot of time by herself," Soonie whispered during a rare quiet moment. "Maybe the talking will work itself out after a few days."

Despite Mrs. William's dire predictions that they would all 'catch the monia' from sleeping in the small tent, the four women were so tired by the time they went to bed that no chill could have kept them awake. Not even the loud snores from the men outside disturbed their slumber.

True to his word, Mr. Humphries assigned two men to work on the shelter. Under the watchful eye of Mrs. Dawson, they completed a decent lean-to and a separate kitchen in two days.

The women managed to scrape together meals with the limited supplies on hand, while planning better menus for the next week. The fourth night, Wylder surprised them with a deer he had shot on the way back to camp.

Though conditions had improved considerably from the first day, Zillia was very thankful to climb into the wagon and head back to the train on Friday afternoon. She missed Orrie so much she ached. Though Soonie was with her, seeing Wylder's sullen face every day, at every meal caused her heart to ache even more.

14

The Toppled Giant

An errant wind pulled at the treetops. Branches, brittle from past droughts, snapped and scattered on the forest floor. Some fell with loud cracks against the lean-to's roof.

Mrs. Williams closed her eyes and clasped her hands in front of her. "Lord have mercy on us! If there's a storm, this whole building will probably come crashing down upon our heads. Oh, I do wish it was afternoon so I could go home!"

"I don't." Zillia stirred a kettle of stew. "What if we were in the wagon and a storm hit? Or on the train? Can a train even travel through a storm?"

"I'm not sure." Soonie paused from kneading bread dough. The sticky substance hung from her fingers in clumps. "But it will pass soon. These early summer storms never last long."

"But they can be violent. Grandpa Walt lost the windmill last year when the weather was just like this," Zillia pointed out.

"Ladies, ladies, we're going to be fine!" Mrs. Dawson bustled in with a basket of potatoes. "Let's focus on the tasks in front of us."

Zillia tasted the stew. The spicy venison and fresh vegetables were cooked to perfection. "It's ready." She ladled the steaming liquid into large pails.

Soonie filled baskets with golden squares of cornbread. Each woman took what they could carry and hurried to the breezy outdoors.

Mr. Humphries had requested they bring the lunch out to where the men were working for the next few days. The crew was trying to get a section cleared by the end of the week.

"Now I know what a pack mule feels like," Mrs. Williams struggled with her heavy bucket. Her shawl whipped around her shoulders.

"The men aren't far. They had to take all the wagons today to try to get the area finished up." Mrs. Dawson said, though her own face was red and her shoulders sagged under her burden. "We'll be back at the camp in no time."

Zillia and Soonie exchanged smiles. Over the past few weeks, they had become accustomed to the women's contradicting attitudes.

Soon bright jackets moving through the trees let them know

they had almost reached the men's work area.

Zillia sat down her pails to rub her neck. Dark shadows crept over the skies and a chill settled over the forest.

Soonie shaded her eyes. "Goodness! What a monster."

A massive pine creaked ahead of them. Axes bit into the trunk, creating a raw wound like a mouth, open in a silent scream.

"Why aren't they using a misery whip?" Zillia pointed to the supply wagon, where the thin, long saws were kept.

"Wylder said they dull faster than you can think," Soonie said. "It takes hours to sharpen them again. They're miserable to use, that's how they got the name."

Mr. Humphries caught sight of the women and hurried over. "We're gonna chop this tree afore we eat. You ladies stand over there, out of the way. We'll be with ya in a coon's wink." He pointed to a distant clump of stumps.

"Happy to oblige." Mrs. Dawson scurried over to the spot and set down her buckets. She kneaded her hands together. "That does smart."

A loud creak announced that the mighty pine, had almost given up its fight.

Most of the men came across the gully to stand by the women.

Abel and Wylder stood on little platforms wedged several feet up into the tree's trunk to finish the last blows. Two other men stood by to help them down from the platforms when they were finished.

A man leaned toward Zillia. "At's a dangerous job, right der.

Only the young and spry ones stay up for the last blows."

Breezes tugged at Zillia's hair, blowing it all around her face in a tangle. She pushed it out of her eyes and watched the two figures. Wylder seemed so confident, so sure of himself. *Would he really be up there if it were such a risk?*

A giant gust of wind sailed through the ladies' skirts. The men shouted as hats were torn from their heads.

An unearthly groan from the huge pine tree interrupted the chaos. A shudder ran through the trunk, which teetered and then began to fall in the wrong direction.

Get out of the way. Zillia grabbed Mrs. Dawson's hand and pulled the older woman along through the group of moving bodies. Everyone pushed and shouted, some trying to help, some knocking co-workers down in their haste to reach to safety.

Branches and trunk loomed towards them, smaller trees snapping and breaking under the mighty weight. The very tip of the tree crashed a foot away from Mrs. Williams, who screamed.

Zillia coughed and waved her hands in front of her face, trying to see through the clouds of dirt and bark. People huddled all around her, arms still covering their heads.

"Wylder!" Soonie dropped the basket of bread. She fought through branches to reach the chopped end of the tree.

Zillia stood as though one of the pines, rooted to the ground and unable to move. Her heart pounded a reminder. *Forward. Help.* She darted after her friend.

The other workers swarmed over the tree like ants, cutting at branches and calling for the missing men.

Zillia pulled at thick limbs, ignoring the needles digging into her skin. Her shin throbbed where she had bashed it against tree trunk during her flight. *Where is Wylder?*

Then came a voice from the farther side, close to the chop site. "Over here! Help me!" Wylder tugged at Abel's motionless figure.

Blood trickled from a cut on Wylder's cheek in a jagged stream. He was covered in dust.

Soonie reached his side and tugged on his arm. "Are you all right? Are you hurt?"

Zillia couldn't tear her eyes away from Abel. His face was ashen. The same hue Mama's face had turned while her lifeblood drained from her body. And Zillia knew why. A dark stain spread across the man's bright orange shirt.

She clawed at the thick mackinaw until the fabric fell away to reveal a burly chest. A stick's sharp point had worked into the man's flesh.

"We had to jump." Wylder's eyes were wide, and his breathing heavy. "Abel made it down, but he tripped while we were running away. I tried to help him but he'd landed on that spike."

Zillia tried to remove the stick, but the skin held fast, and she worried the loss of blood would be too great. *I must stop the bleeding.* She pulled off her apron and pressed it around the stick with both hands.

Abel's eyes fluttered, and he stared at her for a moment, then closed them again.

"You hang on, Abel Trent. Your mama's already mad enough at me as it is, don't you go dying on my watch!"

Wylder said, "Stay there, Zillia. We have an extra log boat coming; it should be here within an hour if the storm doesn't hold it back. We'll find a way to get him down to the bank."

Big drops of rain splattered against Zillia's shoulders and soaked through her dress. Her hands shook, but she kept the pressure against Abel's skin. As far as she could tell, the flow of blood had stopped.

"God," she prayed out loud, not caring who heard and not taking any chances. "God, don't let this man die. He's not too kind, but please don't let him die. Please."

The warm skin grew cold and the blood soaking the material beneath her fingers dried, stiffening the cloth.

Several men arrived with a stretcher fashioned from poles and two coats. With some effort, Abel was rolled onto the makeshift device. Zillia came with them, moving in swift steps to keep up with the men who carried the stretcher.

After an agonizing half mile through the rain, the miserable party reached the riverbank.

A small overhang in the rocks gave a bit of shelter. The crevasse was a tight squeeze, but dry. The men set Abel down gently. Zillia curled in beside him.

Zillia hadn't seen a response from the injured man since the beginning of the journey, but his chest still rose and fell under her hands.

Soonie's face appeared through the crowd of men. "Are you all right?"

"I'm fine. It's nice to be out of the rain." Zillia tried to squirm into a more comfortable position.

"I'll try to get you something hot to drink." Soonie disappeared before Zillia could tell her not to bother, she didn't have a free hand anyway.

Mr. Humphries knelt down and studied her under bushy eyebrows. "I'm a log man. I don't know nothin' about healing folks. I'm thinkin' you better keep holdin' that wound until the barge gets here."

"Shouldn't they just take the wagon?" Wylder asked.

"Nope. Barge'll cut the time down by four hours, plus it's a smoother trip if the rain lets up."

The acrid scent of blood mixed with the sweat and damp. Zillia shivered. People dropped like June Bugs on a lantern. If not from an accident, by some sickness or plague. Her parents, Soonie's parents, Abel's father, and now Abel. *Why even bother going on with each day? It'll end in some horrible way sooner or later.*

A delicious scent drifted from the opening as Soonie ducked in. "Try to be still, I'll spoon this for you." She held out a tin cup of soup.

Soonie awkwardly tried to scoop the hot liquid into Zillia's mouth and the two girls giggled, despite the situation.

"I feel like Orrie." Zillia said, while Soonie wiped away a stray drop making its way down her chin.

"The barge is here!" came a call from the bank.

Soonie put down the cup of soup. She placed her hands on Abel's forehead, closed her eyes, and murmured in her native tongue.

Zillia caught the words for "God" and "help," so she knew her friend was praying. She couldn't help but smile. *How would Abel feel if he knew Soonie was praying for him in Comanche?*

"We're ready. Let's go." Mr. Humphries gestured to his crew.

When Zillia stood, trying to stretch muscles that had been cramped for far too long, she felt warmth drape across her shoulders. Wylder's coat. She breathed in his familiar scent.

"Hold tight, Zillia," he whispered in her ear.

The men heaved their burden of flesh onto the boat, with Zillia right beside them.

The boat began to move, and the rain stopped as quickly as it had begun. Sun beamed down through the clouds, creating diamond droplets on the tree branches hanging above the river.

The last thing Zillia heard over the barge's chugging steam engine was Mrs. Williams exclamation of "Glory be!" while the boat slipped around a curve.

###

Hours later, the doctor placed a gentle hand over Zillia's.

"You can let go now, Miss Bright."

Pain buzzed through her fingers as she shook the feeling back into them. She scooted back against the wall, watching the doctor as he bent over the large man on the bed.

Abel stirred, lifted his head and looked around the room with glazed eyes. He sank back down on the ferry owner's cot.

The doctor probed the skin around the stick. "Doesn't appear to have punctured any vitals. But you definitely helped this man by stopping the blood loss."

He adjusted his spectacles and glanced around at the concerned faces of the boat driver and his small crew. "I'll have to operate in here to remove the object. Take this girl somewhere and get her warmed up."

Zillia sank to her knees in relief. "I did it!" she whispered. "With God's help, I saved a Trent!"

Someone knocked on the door. The ferry owner opened it.

"Excuse me, I'm looking for …" Mrs. Fowler caught sight of Zillia. "Oh, you poor thing!" She swept across the room and gathered her into a hug. "You're coming home with me right now."

They crossed the river in a rowboat, then climbed into the Fowler's buggy.

"Everyone is saying you are a hero!" Mrs. Fowler's chin quivered beneath her bonnet's silk bow. "Are you all right? Do you have a chill?"

Zillia drew Wylder's coat tighter. "I'm fine."

"You most certainly are not fine! Imagine us, thinking you were going into a respectable place. Surely they wouldn't allow young, innocent girls into a dangerous area. And there you were, a tree could topple on your head at any moment. And almost did. The very idea!" Mrs. Fowler slapped the reins, and the horse looked back at her reproachfully.

Zillia stared out into the forest. Mrs. Fowler was right. She shouldn't have taken such a risk. She was Orrie's only caretaker. *What would he do if something happened to me?*

A realization hit her, like a sudden ray of sunshine during a storm. Peace filled her heart. and she knew what she needed to do.

Saturday morning, Zillia settled into the soft, cloth-covered chair across from Mr. Ulysses Alder, Attorney at Law.

Mr. Alder's smile covered his face. "What do I owe the pleasure of today's visit, Miss Bright?"

She pulled a paper from her pocket and smoothed it out on the table. "I've decided to sell the farm."

JULY 1889

15

Dark Hour

The scrub-brush knew the floor well. The scratching sound it made while Zillia passed it over the boards was familiar as the song she always sang while doing this tedious chore.

> *"Oh dear, what can the matter be?*
> *Dear, dear, what can the matter be?*
> *O dear, what can the matter be?*
> *Johnny's so long at the fair.*
> *He promised he'd buy me a fairing should please me,*
> *And then for a kiss, oh! he vowed he would tease me,*
> *He promised he'd bring me a bunch of blue ribbons,*

To tie up my bonny brown hair."

Zillia had never cared too much for Johnny. *Poor girl, I suppose her hair wasn't quite bonny enough.*

Rocking back on her heels, she surveyed her work.

Hard to believe she'd never clean this floor again. Tonight was her last night in her parents' home.

Every board had been carefully planned and chosen by Papa. After he died, Mama would sometimes go from room to room to touch a fixture, or lean her head against a wall. Zillia always thought she must be remembering the moments Papa stood in those places, explaining an angle to a foreman or tapping in a nail.

A part of Zillia wanted to cling to the scrub-brush and cry like a little girl. The last thing she possessed that had belonged to both of her parents was about to be wrenched away from her.

Buried in Mama's trunk, under the few remaining articles of clothing she had held back, was the down payment for the house and land. Mr. Alder had delivered it earlier that afternoon. He'd spent several days going through the law books, but in the end he'd come to a conclusion; Jeb hadn't contacted her in almost three years. By law, he had abandoned any rights to the farm.

Word had surely reached the Trent family, but the only thing she'd heard from Jemima was a stammered thanks for saving Abel's life. She guessed they wouldn't dare try to stop the sale now.

The house was clean as it could be. The buyer would arrive in the morning. Nothing left to do but go to bed, though sleep would be hard to come by. Their few remaining treasures had already been packed up and taken to the boarding house in town where they would stay until she figured out where to go next.

Orrie had been tucked into his little bed hours ago. Gruff slept in the barn for the night, to avoid the introduction of fleas to the house.

Zillia stepped on the porch. Darkness had settled over the farm like a velvet shawl. The stars seemed brighter than ever, but that could have been because of the tears in her eyes. She whisked them away and decided to walk down the bank, to say goodbye to her special bend in the river and all the prayers, hopes and dreams she had spoken there.

The scrub brush. If she didn't remember to dump the bucket tonight, the house might be filled with the sour smell of the wash water. She went back inside and reached for the handle.

The door swung open behind her, and the floorboards creaked. She turned, and her heart fell to her very knees. She swallowed in an attempt to pull it back up to her chest.

"J–Jeb." she managed to croak.

He stepped into the glow of her lantern's flame. His wiry frame seemed leaner then when she'd last seen him, over three years ago, and a new scar ran up and over his left eye, still red and healing.

Zillia settled back against the table, her fingers searching for a gun, rolling pin, anything. Only bare boards met her skin;

everything useful had already been packed away.

"Look at you," Jeb hissed. One front tooth was gone. "Cozy and comfy in this home while I've traveled the country like a hobo. I've slept in barns and worked like a dog doing jobs you wouldn't even imagine."

"Oh wouldn't I!" The words leapt off her tongue. "I've run this farm and cared for your own flesh and blood for three years. You took everything from us, Jeb!"

"Huh. Everything? Not everything, Missy. I waited in a prison cell through the four seasons three times." He held up three grimy fingers. "For you. To give up and move out. You coulda given Orrie to my sister and gone to live with your kinfolks. Heck, you coulda found a man to take you away from here, if anyone'd put up with your sass. But no, you were too stubborn. And then, what do I hear?" Boots scraped the floor while he took another step closer. "You sell my land. Right out from under me." A string of drool dribbled down from the corner of his mouth.

Zillia remembered the signs all too well. Jeb was drunk. She'd never understood how he could make it all the way from town on horseback in this condition.

"Well, Jeb." She tried to steady her voice. "Mama's bed is up in the attic. Why don't you go get some rest and we can talk about this in the morning?"

In a swift motion, Jeb pulled out a pistol and leveled it at her head. It glimmered, a stark contrast to his shabby clothes and matted hair.

"I'm not going anywhere until you tell me why you sold my property, and where you hid the money. I'd think you'd got at least three dollars an acre. Nice compensatory for all my years of suffering, dontcha think?"

Zillia bit her lip until the bitter taste of blood tickled her tongue. Jeb had no legal right to the money. Mr. Alders had gone over every dot and line to be sure. She couldn't tell her stepfather where she had hidden the gold, the money was all she had for her and Orrie's future.

A whimper from the door made her heart pound faster. Orrie stood in his pajamas, his golden curls standing on end like dandelion puffs. "Zilly, who's that?"

"Is that my boy?" Jeb lowered his pistol a fraction of an inch. "Jeb Junior, is that you?"

"His name is Orrie, you know that." Zillia's fear boiled into rage. "And he's your son by blood only. I've been his only family for three years. You have no claim."

Jeb swung around to face her, darkness seeping into his face. "No claim? No claim, to my own boy?" He staggered over to Orrie and grabbed the little boy's arm.

"Don't you touch him." Zillia darted towards him.

Jeb snapped around to face her. "Don't move. Unless you want to go fetch that gold."

Orrie's face melted and tears puddled in his eyes. "Ow! You're hurting!"

"Jeb, please let him go. I'll get you the money. Please!"

Jeb gestured with the gun. "Hurry up," he grunted.

She rushed through the door, Orrie's sobs following her. *Stay calm. Maybe he'll be happy with the money and leave.*

Jeb stepped over so he could watch her through the doorway. "Keep your hands out!" he barked. "Don't want you pulling out a gun on me or nothin'."

Zillia raised her hands in the air and went to the bedside, where Mama's old chest was ready to be moved out in the morning. "The money is in here," she called over her shoulder.

Jeb yanked Orrie into the room behind her. His hot breath poured down over her shoulder. "Well, open it."

She pulled up the heavy lid and dug through the last few things in the trunk, mostly stained aprons and house dresses Mama never would have worn in public. Underneath was the flour sack, heavy with its twenty ten dollar gold pieces. She pulled it out and dropped it on the floor. "There it is. Take it, and leave us alone."

A dark light flared in Jeb's eyes. He let go of Orrie to open the bag with one hand while clutching his gun in the other.

Orrie stumbled to Zillia and tugged at her skirts, still sobbing. "It's going to be all right," she murmured to her brother while she rubbed his back.

Jeb counted the coins once, then twice. "Finally, something's goin' right for ol' Jeb." He dropped the gold back into the bag and wrapped the twine around it tightly. "After all these years."

"Now for you," he turned back to Zillia. "You're the problem, ain't ya? Always have been." He leveled his gun back at her. "The minute I ride outta here you'll be off to town to blab all about mean ol' Jeb. Even though it's my rightful money."

"No, I won't tell anyone!" Zillia pressed her hand against her heart, sure he could hear it. "Please, Jeb, just leave us alone!"

"Oh, you'd like that, wouldn't ya? But that," he pointed a dirty finger at Orrie. "That's my boy. And I'm taking him with me. I know you won't keep your mouth shut, you never could. You always tattle-taled everything, didn't ya? Now it's over. I'm gonna shut that mouth up forever."

He pulled a length of rope from his pocket and waved it at her. "Go back to the kitchen."

"What are you going to do?" Zillia stepped back into the kitchen without taking her eyes of the man.

"What I should've done three years ago. What I would have done sooner if I hadn't landed in jail. Grab that skillet from the corner over there."

The kettle she used to hold bacon fat. Forgotten in the scurry of packing. She picked it up and held it out to him. "What do you want with this old thing?"

He tossed the rope over to her. "Wrap one end around the handle, then tie the other end around your ankle."

The coarse rope stung her fingers while she obeyed. *Take care of Orrie, take care of Orrie.* This time, she couldn't pray the words out loud. Tears burned the corners of her eyes, but she would not let Jeb see her cry.

She finished and stood up, holding the heavy kettle. A few feet of rope hung slack to her ankle.

Jeb nodded toward the door. "Now, let's get outside. You always did like the river, didn't ya?"

Zillia's eyes widened. *He's going to shoot me and throw me in.* "No, Jeb, you can't do this. Please!" *What could I bribe him with? What does he care about the most?* "If they find out, they'll hang you."

"No one knows I'm back, and I'm taking the little brat with me. Most folks round here think I'm still in jail or dead anyways."

The tears came, and this time she couldn't hold them in. Her knees wobbled, and she fought to stay on her feet.

Orrie's chin trembled. His mouth opened to wail along with her.

Jeb slapped the little boy across the face, and a bright red spot bloomed on the chubby cheek. "Shut up, kid. You're gonna learn to behave around your pa."

Jeb's head was turned towards Orrie, and for an instant he'd lowered the gun.

Zillia hefted the kettle, the same pan that she'd used for the afterbirth after Orrie was born. One of the only things Jeb had left behind three years ago. She swung the cast iron with every ounce of strength towards Jeb's head.

Jeb pulled up his shoulder just in time to fend off the blow, but she still heard bones crunch. Lowering his head, he charged at her like a wild pig and knocked her to the floor.

The front door burst open, and a dark figure in a long coat

rushed towards Jeb. The man pulled her stepfather away from her and flung him against the wall.

"Zillia, are you hurt?" Wylder held his hand out to her.

"Jeb is armed, watch out!" Zillia struggled to get up.

Wylder swung around while Jeb fumbled for his weapon. Wylder stomped down on his skittering fingers.

Jeb bellowed in pain.

Wylder twisted Jeb's arm back behind his back. "Attacking women and children now, Jeb?" he hissed. "I guess abandoning them wasn't enough for you?"

Never had Zillia seen Wylder in such a state. A deadly anger swam below a cool mask plastered across his handsome face.

Zillia pulled the rope from her ankle and flung it to the floor, where it lay like a limp snake.

Wylder picked it up and trussed Jeb's hands behind his back. "I should kill you now."

No, no. As much as Zillia hated the man tied up in front of her, she didn't want Wylder to have blood on his hands. He wasn't that kind of person.

"You're a lucky man, Jeb," Wylder continued to tighten the rope around her stepfather's shoulders and arms. "I wouldn't want Orrie to see his father's death. God will be your judge."

Jeb said nothing, but his eyes shot venomous darts at both of them.

"Are you all right?" Wylder reached out to help her once again.

"Y—yes." Zillia struggled to her feet. Sore places announced themselves all over her body.

"I'm going to need you to come with me to town," Wylder said. "You'll have to drive the wagon while I make sure this piece of filth keeps quiet. We'll get the doctor to check you over when we get there. Do you think you can manage?"

Zillia nodded. "Wylder..."

He reached out and cupped her chin with his hand. "Just breathe for now." He smiled his lopsided smile. "Everything's going to be all right. Go get the wagon ready. Don't think about anything else."

She took Orrie's hand. "Did you hear that? Let's go on an adventure, Orrie."

Orrie turned up a face still streaked with tears. Trust filled his eyes. "Can we send the bad man away?"

"Yes, Orrie. He will never bother us again."

Wylder pounded on the door of the sheriff's house. "Sheriff, it's an emergency."

The door creaked open and the sheriff stepped out in his long johns. "I hope this is good." He followed Wylder out to the wagon and held up his lantern. "Well, well, well. Jeb Bowen. And Zillia Bright. Interesting party you've brought to me, Mr. Eckhart. I'm sure you have a bedtime story to go along with it?"

Wylder nodded. "That I do, Sheriff, but I'd be more comfortable telling it if this man were in a cell."

"Let me get some pants." The sheriff disappeared back into his house.

An hour later, Jeb was safely locked away. After Zillia had told her story, the sheriff scooted back his chair. "It won't be a hanging offence, and more's the pity. But since your young man here," he pointed to Wylder, "witnessed the attack, Mr. Bowen will be in jail for a very long time. You won't have to worry about him again."

"No, she won't." Wylder's eyes held an intensity Zillia had never seen. "Will that be all you need from us tonight?"

"Yep." The sheriff smiled down at Orrie, who had fallen asleep on Zillia's lap. "Make sure these folks get home."

Wylder scooped Orrie up gently with one arm, and took Zillia's hand with his free one. "That I'll do, sheriff. We're heading to the doctor's next."

Zillia sighed. "I'm fine. Can we please just go home, Wylder? I'm so tired."

Wylder searched her face for a moment. "All right."

Once outside, he placed the sleeping boy on a pile of flour sacks in the wagon.

He climbed next to Zillia. After twisting the reins around his hands, he pulled her fingers into the tangle and held them tight. He didn't say anything.

And she didn't try to pull away, just held on, as though for dear life.

Stars burned through tree branches. Unseen creatures played their symphony in praise of the night. Wylder murmured something. At first, Zillia thought he was praying, but a melody soon emerged.

"Let every flower, every star
be blessed,
Let every traveler coming far
find rest"

The words came in a clear tenor, which rose and fell over the rattling wagon wheels and the jingle of the tack. Words of a song unfamiliar to Zillia. *This must be a song he wrote, for God, like Soonie told me about.* A peace settled over her, like she had never felt. And a knowledge. *God is here. With us.* Her eyes widened, and she wanted to ask Wylder if he felt the same way. His eyes shone in the moonlight, and a tear trickled down his cheek. *He knows.*

Zillia snuggled into Wylder's shoulder and closed her eyes. He drew a sharp breath, then arranged the reins so he could pull her closer.

"Let the light of God
pour into your heart,

and find blessings and peace, this night."

16 Light of Day

"Zilly, I want breakfast *now*."

Pain. Not piercing, but in dull patches all over her body. Zillia sat up and clutched her head. "Orrie, you'd want breakfast on judgement day, even if Gabriel blew his horn."

Her arm was peppered with bruises, in colors she'd never seen before. She stared at it for a moment. Then she remembered. "The buyers are going to be here this morning!"

She jumped out of bed and yanked her dress down from the hook beside it. Spots pricked the air in front of her eyes. Swaying for a moment, she finally had to sink down on the bed again.

"You coming?" Orrie pushed his head through the crook of her arm and peered up at her.

"Yes, yes. I'm coming."

After taking several extra moments to get dressed, Zillia finally made it into the kitchen. She stared at the floor in dismay. Furniture was overturned and out of place. Muddy footprints covered the floor, and grease from the skillet had splattered everything in the room. *The buyer will just have to understand. If they'll give me a few extra days, maybe I can get it cleaned up.*

Fortunately, the covered dish on top of the pie safe hadn't been disturbed. She pulled out one of the biscuits she had put aside for their breakfast and plunked it down in front of Orrie. "Here you go."

He scrunched up his face. "Can I have butter?"

"May I have butter?" Zillia reminded him. She went into the pantry to find the container.

Waves of panic, leftover from the night before, swept over her. *If Wylder hadn't come—*

She'd be at bottom the river right now, the sunlight filtering through the water's surface and into her sightless eyes. "I can't think about this." She leaned against the pantry shelf and took a deep breath. For whatever reason, Wylder had come. *I have today.*

Was it all a dream? After the third time of having to sit and collect herself, she stood and shook her head. Not today. She could work through this later. The buyers would arrive at any time.

While smoothing her hair, an envelope on the mantelpiece caught her eye. "Where did this come from?" Zillia flattened out the crinkled, stained paper.

"Wylder put it there," Orrie said.

"Oh. So that's what brought him out last night." Whatever the letter was about, it had saved her life. She squinted at the return address but the writing had been smudged in its travels. "I don't know who it's from, Orrie."

She opened the inside paper. The script was fancy and small, but she knew it in an instant. Her heart skipped a beat.

"My Dearest Zillia,

We have wondered and worried for you and your mother this long while. It is with great sadness we learned of Marjorie's death, from Mrs. Gerta Fowler. We do not understand why you couldn't write of this news with your own hand.

Grandfather Thomas is well and sends you his love. Aunt Clara's sons have gone to University and she has begged for you to bring the baby and come to live here, in Alexandria. We shudder to imagine the difficult times you must have gone through in the past few years. If we had only known, we would have sent for you much sooner.

Please come on the swiftest train,
Your Grandmother Bright."

Two ten-dollar bills fell into Zillia's hand. She stared at the money. The date on the letter stated January 15th, 1889.

They must have written this when I lived with Mrs. Fowler. Why did it take so long to get here? And why didn't Mrs. Fowler tell me she had written to them? The letter could have been lost somewhere along the route, and then found again. As for the second question-- *Mrs. Fowler probably didn't want me to be disappointed if no answer came.*

Could she go back to the world of corsets and bustles, of gloves every day and curtsies and afternoon tea? She inhaled sharply. *Do I want to live with people who rejected my mother for so long?*

Orrie touched the paper. "What's it say, Zilly?"

Her brother deserved a good life, with warm clothes and plenty of food and the care her eastern relatives could afford to give. But how would he do in fancy schools, forced to wear starched collars and pantaloons? She almost laughed out loud at the thought of her little ragamuffin as a city slicker.

Gruff barked from the yard. Several horses clattered up into the yard. She hobbled to the door.

Confusion fluttered through her heart when she caught sight of the three riders. She knew Mr. Alder brought the paperwork, but why...

Wylder dismounted and reached her side first. "Are you all right?" he studied her face. From the hollows under his eyes, she knew he had stayed and guarded the property throughout the night.

"I will be." She looked away. "I'm trying not think about it."

His hand settled on her shoulder. "Everything's going to be fine."

She stumbled and clutched at his coat. And now she was sobbing. Deep, racking sobs that came from a place inside of herself, where she had stored all her fears and sadness the last three years. A place locked up tight. Now the dam broke open, and the torrent flowed through.

Wylder held her awkwardly at first, and then his arms grew tighter and he stroked her hair, the way she did for Orrie when he was sad.

Boots crunched the gravel. Grandpa Walt and Mr. Alder must have moved off to tie their horses up.

Finally, her sobs turned into hiccups and she drew back.

Wylder wiped her tears away with his thumb and smiled down at her. "Better?"

Zillia nodded. Even through her tears, she saw a gleam in his eye. It had been there the night of the dance, the day he fished her out of the river. On Sundays when she saw him at church. Wylder loved her. Loved her more than for friendship, loved her despite her faults, despite her situation.

"L—look at you." Zillia rubbed the large damp spot that had formed on his coat. "You're a mess. And me! I must be a fright! The buyer will be here at any second! Oh, what will they think of me?"

Ulysses and Grandpa Walt began to chuckle, and Wylder's mouth turned up at the corners below his moustache.

"Sorry for laughing." Grandpa Walt put his hand on her shoulder. "We are the buyers."

Her hands flew to her mouth to stifle a gasp. "What did you say?"

"Grandma Louise and I have always wanted to live closer to the river. With a little work, this house would be warmer, and it's bigger than our cabin. We still have two growing boys to raise. We've been saving back a long time, and were looking at another spot, but when you decided to sell, we just couldn't let it go to a stranger. We wanted it to be a surprise."

"Who will buy your homestead?" was all Zillia could think to say.

"I am," Wylder replied. "It's a cozy place, and good soil. It's time I start running my own farm. That's why I went to work at the lumber camp, so I could put some money down on the place."

"How wonderful!" Zillia felt like throwing her arms around his neck, but she had made quite enough of a spectacle already. "You've been wanting that your whole life."

Wylder glanced up at her, and then turned his head away, but not before she saw his huge grin. "Yep."

With trembling fingers, Zillia straightened her apron. Her hand closed over the crumpled bills in her pocket. Her shoulders sagged. "I might be going east, with Orrie." The decision weighed on her, but what could she do? *It's the only way.*

The light dimmed in Wylder's eyes. "I had a feeling that's what the letter would be about. Didn't even want to bring it over. I don't know why I picked last night to deliver it."

"I'm glad you did." Zillia shuddered.

"So am I, considering."

Grandpa Walt cleared his throat. "Folks, I hate to interrupt, but Mr. Alder is a busy man. Why don't we continue this conversation after we get everything settled with the house?"

Zillia stared at Grandpa Walt. She had almost forgotten the other two men were there. "Oh, of course. I beg your pardon."

"Not a problem at all, ma'am." Mr. Alder bowed, and they all went inside.

A short time later, the last of Zillia's belongings were packed into the wagon. The wooden rocker she had rocked Orrie to sleep in almost every night. Mama's trunk with its sentimental treasures. The (now cleaned) skillet she couldn't bear to part with. She walked through the hollow rooms. *How do you say goodbye to a life?* At least she knew Grandpa Walt and Grandma Louise would love and care for the home.

Finally, she stepped outside and walked down to her favorite rock. She stood still, listening to the river flow over the rocks.

Wylder came to stand beside her. "Orrie's almost asleep. You might as well stay here one more night. Grandpa won't mind."

.She shook her head. "The Fowlers will have supper for us, and the boarding room expects me. After last evening, I don't want to be by myself anymore."

Wylder took her hand then, cradling her fingers as though they were made of fine china. "Zillia, I know Virginia would offer you a better, more comfortable future. You would never have to work in the fields again, or cook over a hot stove in the Texas heat. So what I'm going to ask is selfish and crazy. But I can't let you go away without asking."

"You don't have a selfish bone in your body, Wylder Eckhart."

"Well, you might think differently after I ask my question. I want you to stay, Zillia."

"Why?" Zillia stared up into his blue, blue eyes. "What do I have here?"

"Well, you have Soonie. And the Fowlers, they're nice. Our general store has the best cider in the state. And I doubt the royal palace of England can put on a dance as good as the Town Improvement Society."

"Yes, that's true, but—"

"And me. You have me." His eyes glimmered again, and no more words were needed. He gently lifted her chin and covered her lips with his own.

Warmth. Love. Comfort. Zillia hadn't brought herself to hope for these feelings since Mama died. A lifetime of sorrow washed off her shoulders and fell into the dust around her feet.

Wylder finally drew back. "I don't have much more to offer than what you have lived with the past three years." He traced the curve of her chin with his finger. "We'll still have the farm struggles. The dirt and the hard work."

"But—we'll have us," Zillia said quietly. "That's more than I could ever want."

He kissed her once more, and the river rushed on, singing a new song just for them.

The End

About the Author

Angela has been writing stories since she created her first book with a green crayon at the age of eight. She's lived all over Central Texas, mostly hovering in and around the small town of Bastrop Texas, which she loves with unnatural fierceness and features in many of her books. Angela has four wild children, a husband who studies astrophysics for fun, and a cat.
To find out more about her writing and learn how to receive a FREE short story, go to
http://angelacastillowrites.weebly.com

Made in United States
Troutdale, OR
09/02/2024